No one writes romantic fiction like Barbara Cartland.

Miss Cartland was originally inspired by the best of the romantic novelists she read as a girl —writers such as Elinor Glyn, Ethel M. Dell and E. M. Hull. Convinced that her own wide audience would also delight in her favorite authors, Barbara Cartland has taken their classic tales of romance and specially adapted them for today's readers.

Bantam is proud to publish these novels—personally selected and edited by Miss Cartland— under the imprint

**BARBARA CARTLAND'S
LIBRARY OF LOVE**

Bantam Books by Barbara Cartland
Ask your bookseller for the books you have missed

Barbara Cartland's Library of Love series

Barbara Cartland's Ancient Wisdom series

Barbara Cartland's
Library of Love
Freckles
by Gene Stratton Porter

Condensed by Barbara Cartland

BANTAM BOOKS
TORONTO · NEW YORK · LONDON

FRECKLES
A Bantam Book / *December 1978*

ISBN 0–553–12392–0

Published simultaneously in the United States and Canada

Bantam Books are published by Bantam Books, Inc. Its trademark, consisting of the words "Bantam Books" and the por-
trayal of a bantam, is Registered in U.S. Patent and Trademark
Office and in other countries. Marca Registrada. Bantam
Books, Inc., 666 Fifth Avenue, New York, New York 10019.

PRINTED IN THE UNITED STATES OF AMERICA

Introduction

This is a tender love-story that is impossible to forget.

With a hero who tugs at one's heart-strings, an Angel of whom he dreams, and cruel, ruthless villains, the story is set in the wild swampland of the Limberlost, the toughest, most frightening place in America, and the most beautiful.

Read about Freckles and love him. It is impossible not to!

So, being among these beautiful things every day,

Chapter
One

Freckles came down the trail that crossed the lower end of the Limberlost. At a glance he might have been mistaken for a tramp, but he was truly seeking work.

Long before he came in sight of the camp of the Grand Lumber Company, he could hear the cheery voices of the men and the neighing of the horses, and could scent the tempting odours of cooking food.

The thickness of the swamp made a dark, massive background below; above, gigantic trees towered. The men were calling jovially back and forth as they unharnessed tired horses that fell into attitudes of rest and began to crunch, in deep content, the grain given them.

Duncan, the brawny Scottish head-teamster, lovingly wiped the flanks of his big bays as he softly whistled, *"O wha' will be, my dearie O!"*

Wreathing tongues of flame wrapped round the big black kettles. When the cook lifted the lids to plunge in his testing-fork, gusts of savoury odours escaped.

Freckles approached him.

"I want to speak with the Boss," he said.

The cook glanced at him and answered carelessly:

"He can't use you."

The colour flooded Freckles' face, but he said simply:

"If you will be having the goodness to point him out, we will give him a chance to do his own talking."

With a shrug of astonishment, the cook led the way to a rough board table where a broad, square-shouldered man was bending over some account-books.

"Mr. McLean, here's another man wanting to be taken on the gang, I suppose," he said.

"All right," came the cheery answer. "I never needed a good man more that I do just now."

The Manager turned a page and carefully began a new line.

"No use of your bothering with this fellow," volunteered the cook. "He hasn't but one hand."

The flush on Freckles' face burned deeper. His lips thinned to a mere line as he lifted his shoulders, took a step forward, and thrust out his right arm, from which dangled the sleeve, empty at the wrist.

"That will do, Sears," came the voice of the Boss sharply. "I will interview my man when I finish this report."

He returned to his work while the cook hurried to the fires.

Freckles stood for one instant as he had braced himself to meet the eyes of the Manager; then his arm dropped and a wave of hope swept him.

The Boss had not even turned his head. He had used the possessive when he had said, "my man," and the hungry heart of Freckles had gone reaching towards him.

The boy drew a quivering breath. Then he whipped off his old hat and beat the dust from it carefully. With his left hand he caught the right sleeve, wiped his sweaty face, and tried to straighten his hair with his fingers.

The Boss, busy over his report, was nevertheless vaguely alive to the toilette being made behind him, which he felt scored one for the man.

McLean was a Scotsman. It was his habit to work slowly and methodically. The men of his camps never had known him to be in a hurry or to lose his temper. Discipline was inflexible, but the Boss was always kind.

His habits were simple. He shared camp with his gangs, and the only visible signs of wealth consisted of a big, shimmering diamond stone of ice and fire that glittered and burned on one of his fingers, and the dainty, beautiful thoroughbred mare he rode between camps and across the country on business.

No man of McLean's gangs could honestly say that he had ever been overdriven or underpaid. The Boss had never exacted any deference from his men, yet so intense was his personality that no man among them had ever attempted a familiarity.

They all knew him to be a thorough gentle-man, and that in the great timber-city several millions stood to his credit.

When McLean turned from his finished re-port, he faced a young man, still under twenty, tall, spare, heavily framed, closely freckled, and red-haired, with a homely Irish face.

In the steady grey eyes which were straightly meeting his searching ones of blue there was un-swerving candour and the appearance of longing not to be ignored.

He was dressed in the roughest of farm-clothing and seemed tired to the point of fall-ing.

"You are looking for work?" questioned Mc-Lean.

"Yes, Sir," answered Freckles.

"I am very sorry," said the Boss, with genu-ine sympathy in his every tone, "but there is only one man I want at present—a hardy, big fellow with a stout heart and a strong body. I hoped that you would do, but I am afraid you are too young and scarcely strong enough."

Freckles stood, hat in hand, watching Mc-Lean.

"And what was it you thought I might be doing?" he asked.

The Boss scarcely could repress a start. Sometime before accident and poverty, there had been an ancestor who used cultivated English, even with an accent.

The boy spoke in a mellow Irish voice, sweet and pure. It was scarcely definite enough to be called brogue, yet there was a trick in the turn-ing of the sentence that was almost irresistible to McLean.

"It's no child's job," answered McLean. "I am the Field-Manager of a big lumber company. We have just leased two thousand acres of the Limberlost.

"Many of these trees are of great value. We can't leave our camp, six miles south, for almost a year yet, so we have blazed a trail and strung barbed-wire securely round this lease.

"Before we return to our work," he went on, "I must put this property in the hands of a reliable, brave, strong man who will guard it every hour of the day and sleep with one eye open at night. I intend to require that the entire length of the trail be walked at least twice each day, to make sure that our lines are up and that no one has been trespassing."

Freckles was leaning forward, absorbing every word with such intense eagerness that he was beguiling the Boss into explanations he had never intended to make.

"But why wouldn't that be the finest job in the world for me?" he pleaded. "I am never sick. I could walk the trail twice or three times every day, and I'd be watching sharp all the while."

"You are scarcely more than a boy," answered McLean, "and this job will be trying even for a work-hardened man.

"You see, in the first place, you would be afraid. In stretching our lines, we killed six rattlesnakes almost as big as your body and as thick as your arm.

"It's the price of your life to start through the marsh-grass surrounding the swamp unless you are covered with heavy leather above your knees.

"You should be able to swim in case high

water undermines the temporary bridge we have
built where Sleepy Snake Creek enters the
swamp.

"The fall and winter changes of weather are
abrupt and severe, and I would want strict watch
kept every day. You would always be alone, and
I don't guarantee what is in the Limberlost.

"Worst of all," he continued, "any man who
will enter the swamp to mark and steal timber is
desperate. One of my employees at the South
Camp compelled me to discharge him for a
number of serious reasons.

"He came here, entered the swamp alone,
and succeeded in locating and marking a number
of valuable trees that he was endeavouring to sell
to a rival company when we secured the lease."

McLean paused and looked at the boy.

"He has sworn to have these trees if he has
to die or to kill others to get them; and he is a
man that even the strongest would not care to
meet."

"But if he came to steal trees, wouldn't he
bring teams and men? And wouldn't that mean
that all anyone could do would be to watch and
be able to warn you?" Freckles asked.

"Yes," replied McLean.

"Then why couldn't I be watching just as
closely, and running just as fast, as an older,
stronger man?"

"Why, by George, you could!" exclaimed
McLean. "I don't know as the size of a man would
be half so important as his grit and faithfulness,
come to think of it. Sit on that log there and we
will talk it over. What is your name?"

Freckles shook his head at the proffer of a
seat, and, folding his arms, stood straight as the

trees round him. He grew a shade whiter, but his eyes never faltered.

"Freckles!"

"Good enough for everyday," McLean said, laughing, "but I could scarcely put 'Freckles' on the company's books. Tell me your name."

"I haven't any name."

"I don't understand," said McLean.

"I was thinking from the voice and the face of you that you wouldn't," said Freckles slowly. "I've spent more time on it than I ever did anything else in all my life, and I don't understand.

"Does it seem sense to you that anyone would take a new-born baby and row over it until it was bruised black, cut off its hand, and leave it out in a bitter night on the steps of a Charity Home? That's what somebody did to me."

McLean stared, aghast. He had no reply ready, and presently in a low voice he questioned:

"And after—?"

"The Home people took me in, and I was there till I was the full legal age and several years over. For the most part we were a lot of little Irishmen together. They could always find homes for the other children, but nobody would ever be wanting me, on account of my arm."

"Go on," said McLean, nodding comprehendingly.

"There's nothing worth the taking of your time to tell," replied Freckles. "The Home was in Chicago, and I was there all my life until three months ago.

"When I was too old for the training they gave to the little children, they sent me to the closest ward-school for as long as the law would let them; but I was never like any of the other children, and they all knew it.

"I had to go and come like a prisoner, and be working round the Home early and late for my board and clothes. I always wanted to learn mighty bad, but I was glad when that was over.

"Every few days, all my life, I'd be called up, looked over, and refused a home and love, on account of my hand and ugly face; but it was all the home I'd ever known, and I didn't seem to belong anyplace else.

"Then a new Superintendent was put in. He wasn't for being like any of the others, and he swore he'd weed me out the first thing he did.

"He made a plan to send me down the State to a man he said he knew who had a son and wanted another boy. He wasn't for remembering to tell that man that I was a hand short, and the man knocked me down the minute he found out I was the boy who had been sent to him.

"Between noon and that evening, he and his son had me in pretty much the same shape in which I was found in the beginning, so I lay awake that night and ran away.

"I'd like to have squared my account with the son before I left, but I didn't dare, for fear of waking the old man, and I knew I couldn't handle the two of them; but I'm hoping to meet the boy alone someday before I die."

McLean tugged at his moustache to hide the smile on his lips; he liked Freckles all the better for this confession.

"I didn't even have to steal clothes to avoid starting in my Home ones," Freckles continued, "for they had already taken all my clean, neat things for the boy and put me into his rags, and that went almost as sore as the beatings, for where I was we were always kept tidy and sweet-smelling, anyway.

"I hustled clear into this State before I learned that that man couldn't have kept me if he'd wanted to. When I thought I was good and away from him, I commenced hunting for work, but it is with everybody else just as it is with you, Sir. Big, strong, whole men are the only ones wanted."

"I have been thinking over this matter," replied McLean. "I am sure that a man no older than you and similar in every way could do this work very well, if he was not a coward and had it in him to be trustworthy and industrious."

Freckles came forward a step.

"If you will give me a job where I can earn my food, clothes, and a place to sleep," he said, "if I can have a Boss to work for like other men, and a place I feel I've a right to, I will do precisely what you tell me or die trying."

He said it so quietly and convincingly that McLean believed him, although in his heart he knew that to employ a stranger would be wretched business for a man with the interests he had involved.

"Very well," the Boss found himself answering, "I will enter you on my payrolls. We'll have supper, and then I will provide you with clean clothing, wading-boots, the wire-mending apparatus, and a revolver.

"First thing in the morning, I will take you the length of the trail myself and explain fully what I want done."

His eyes were on the boy as he added quietly:

"All I ask of you is to come to me at once at the South Camp and tell me as a man if you find this job too hard for you. It will not surprise me. It is work that few men would perform faithfully. What name shall I put down?"

Freckles' gaze never left McLean's face, and the Boss saw the swift spasm of pain that swept his lonely, sensitive face.

"I haven't any name," he said stubbornly. "I don't know what mine is and I never will; but I am going to be your man and do your work, and I'll be glad to answer to any name you choose to call me."

His voice was pleading as he said:

"Won't you please be giving me a name, Mr. McLean?"

The Boss wheeled abruptly and began stacking his books. With his eyes still downcast, and in a voice harsh with huskiness, he replied:

"I will tell you what we will do, my lad. My father was my ideal man, and I loved him better than any other I have ever known. He died five years ago, but I believe he would have been proud to leave you his name."

He paused before adding slowly:

"If I give to you the name of my nearest kin and the man I loved best—will that do?"

Freckles' rigid attitude relaxed suddenly. His head dropped, and big tears splashed on the soiled calico shirt.

McLean was not surprised at the silence, for he too found that talking came none too easily just then.

"All right," he said. "I will write it on the roll—James Ross McLean."

"Thank you mightily, Sir," said Freckles. "That makes me feel almost as if I belong already."

"You do," said McLean. "Until someone armed with every right comes to claim you, you are mine. Now, come and take a bath, have some supper, and go to bed."

As Freckles followed him into the lights and sounds of the camp, his heart and soul were singing for joy.

      *   *   *

The next morning found Freckles in clean, whole clothing, fed, and rested. McLean fitted him out and gave him careful instruction in the use of his weapon.

The Boss showed him round the timber-line, and engaged him a place to board, with the family of his head-teamster, Duncan, whom he had brought from Scotland with him and who lived in a small clearing which he was working out between the swamp and the trail.

When the gang started for the South Camp, Freckles was left to guard a fortune in the Limberlost. That he was under guard himself those first weeks he never knew.

Each hour was torture to the boy. The restricted life of a great City Orphanage was the other extreme of the world compared with the Limberlost.

He was afraid for his life every minute. The heat was intense. The heavy wading-boots rubbed his feet until they bled. He was sore and stiff from his long trampings and the outdoor exposure. The seven miles of trail was agony at every step.

At night, under the direction of Duncan, he practised until he grew sure in the use of his revolver. He cut a stout hickory cudgel, with a knot on the end as big as his fist, and it never left his hand.

His heart stood still every time he saw the beautiful marsh-grass begin a sinuous waving *against* the play of the wind, as McLean had told him it would. And he bolted a half-mile with the first boom of the bitterns.

The first afternoon that he found his wires down, and he was compelled to plunge knee-deep into the black swamp-muck to restring them, he became so ill from fear and nervousness that he scarcely could control his shaking hand to do the work.

With every step he felt that he would miss secure footing and be swallowed in that clinging sea of blackness.

In dumb agony he plunged forward, clinging to the posts and trees until he had finished restringing and testing the wire.

Night closed in. The Limberlost stirred gently, then shook herself, growled, and awoke round him.

There seemed to be a great owl hooting from every tree-hollow and a little one screeching from every knot-hole. The bellowing of monster bullfrogs was not sufficiently deafening to shut out the wailing of whippoorwills, which seemed to come from every bush.

Night-hawks swept past him with their shivering cry and bats struck his face. A prowling wild-cat missed its catch and screamed with rage. A straying fox bayed incessantly for its mate.

The hair on the back of Freckles' neck rose as bristles, and his knees wavered beneath him. He stood motionless in an agony of fear. The sweat ran down his face and body in little streams.

Sounds that curdled his blood seemed to encompass him. Fear had so gained the mastery that he did not dare look behind him.

Just when he felt that he would fall dead before he ever reached the clearing, there came Duncan's tolling call:

"Freckles! Freckles!"

A shuddering sob burst from the boy's dry throat. But he only told Duncan that finding the wire down had caused the delay.

The next morning he started on time. Day after day, with his heart pounding, he ducked, dodged, ran when he could, and fought when he was brought to bay. If he ever had an idea of giving up, no one knew it, for he clung to his job without a shadow of wavering.

Duncan, who had been set to watch the first weeks of Freckles' work, carried all these things, insofar as he guessed them, to the Boss at the South Camp. But the innermost, exquisite torture of the thing the big Scotsman never guessed, while McLean, with his finer perceptions, came a little closer.

After a few weeks, when Freckles learned that he was still living, that he had a home, and that the very first money he ever had possessed was safe in his pockets, he began to grow proud.

He still side-stepped, dodged, and hurried to

avoid being late again, but he was gradually developing the fearlessness that men ever acquire of dangers to which they are hourly accustomed.

His heart seemed to be leaping when his first rattler disputed the trail with him, but he mustered courage to attack it with his club.

After its head had been crushed, he mastered his Irishman's inborn repugnance for snakes sufficiently to cut off its rattles to show to Duncan. With this victory, his greatest fear of them was gone.

Then he began to realise that with the abundance of food in the swamp, flesh-hunters would not come on the trail and attack him, and he had his revolver for defence if they did.

He soon learned to laugh at the big, floppy birds that made horrible noises.

One day, watching from behind a tree, he saw a crane solemnly performing a few measures of a belated nuptial song and dance with his mate. Realising that the act was intended in tenderness, no matter how it appeared, the lonely, starved heart of the boy sympathised with them.

Before the first month passed he was fairly easy about his job, and by the next he rather liked it.

When day after day the only thing that relieved his utter loneliness was the companionship of the birds and beasts of the swamp, it was the most natural thing in the world that Freckles should turn to them for friendship.

He began by instinctively protecting the weak and the helpless. He was astonished at the quickness with which they became accustomed to him and the disregard that they showed for his movements.

They learned that he was not a hunter and that the club he carried was used more frequently for their benefit than for his own.

Then when black frosts began stripping the Limberlost, cutting the ferns, shearing the vines from the trees, mowing the succulent green vegetation of the swale, and setting the leaves swirling down, he watched the departing troops of his friends with dismay, and he scarcely could believe what he saw.

He began to realise that he was going to be left alone. He made special efforts towards friendliness, with the hope that he could induce some of them to stay.

It was then that he conceived the idea of carrying food to the birds, for he saw that they were leaving for lack of it. But he could not stop them. Day after day, flocks gathered and departed.

By the time the first snow whitened his trail round the Limberlost, there were left only the little black-and-white juncos, the sapsuckers, the yellow-hammers, a few patriarchs among the flaming cardinals, the blue jays, the crows, and the quail.

The snow fell, covering the swamp, and food was very scarce and difficult to find.

Freckles began his wizard work. He cleared a space of swale, and twice a day he spread a birds' banquet.

The birds scarcely waited until Freckles' back was turned to attack his provisions. In a few weeks they began to fly towards the clearing to meet him.

During the bitter weather of January they came halfway to the cabin every morning and fluttered round him as doves all the way to the feeding-ground.

Before February they were so accustomed to him, and so hunger-driven, that they would perch on his head and shoulders, and the saucy jays would try to pry into his pockets.

Freckles added to the wheat and crumbs every scrap of refuse food he could find at the cabin.

One morning, coming to his feeding-ground unusually early, he found a gorgeous cardinal and a rabbit, side by side, sociably nibbling a cabbage-leaf.

That gave him the idea of cracking nuts, from the store he had gathered for Duncan's children, for the squirrels, in the effort to add them to his family.

So the winter passed. Every week McLean rode to the Limberlost, but never on the same day or at the same hour. Always he found Freckles at his work, faithful and brave, no matter how severe the weather.

The boy's earnings constituted his first money; and when the Boss explained to him that he could leave it safely at a bank, he went straight there every pay-day, keeping out barely what was necessary for his board and clothing.

In imitation of McLean, he bought a small pocket account-book, in which he carefully set down every dollar he earned and every penny he spent.

That winter held the first hours of real happiness in Freckles' life. He was free. He was doing a man's work faithfully, through every rigour of rain, snow, and blizzard.

He was gathering a wonderful strength of body, paying his way, and saving money. Every man of the gang and of that locality knew that he was under the protection of McLean, who was a power, and it had the effect of smoothing Freckles' path in many directions.

Mrs. Duncan showed him that individual kindness for which his hungry heart was longing. She had a hot drink ready for him when he came home from a freezing day on the trail.

She knitted him a heavy mitten for his left hand, and devised a way to sew and pad the right sleeve, which protected the maimed arm in bitter weather.

She patched his clothing—frequently torn by the wire—and saved kitchen-scraps for his birds, not because she either knew or cared anything about them but because she herself was close enough to the swamp to be touched by its utter loneliness.

When Duncan laughed at her for this, she retorted:

"My God, mannie, if Freckles hadna the birds and the beasts, he would be always alone."

"How much answer do ye think he gets to his talkin' to them, lass?" Duncan replied with a laugh.

"He gets the answer that keeps the eye bright, the heart happy, and the feet walking faithful the rough path he's set them in," answered Mrs. Duncan earnestly.

Duncan walked away, appearing very thoughtful.

The next morning he gave Freckles an ear of the corn he was shelling for his chickens, and told him to carry it to his "wild chickens" in the Limberlost. Freckles laughed delightedly.

"My chickens!" he said. "Why didn't I ever think of that before? Of course! They are just little, brightly coloured cocks and hens! But 'wild' is wrong. My 'wild chickens' are a good deal tamer than yours here in your yard."

"Hoot, lad!" cried Duncan.

"Make yours alight on your head and eat out of your hands and pockets," challenged Freckles.

"Go and tell your fairy-tales to the wee people! They're juist brash on believin' things," said Duncan. "Ye canna invent any story too big to stop them from callin' for a bigger."

"I dare you to come see!" retorted Freckles.

"Take ye!" said Duncan. "If ye make juist one bird alight on your head or eat from your hand, ye are free to help yoursel' to my corn-crib and wheat-bin the rest of the winter."

Freckles sprang in air and howled in holy joy.

"Oh, Duncan, you're too easy!" he cried. "When will you come?"

"I'll come next Sabbath," said Duncan. "And I'll believe the birds of the Limberlost are tame as barnyard-fowl when I see it, and no sooner!"

After that Freckles always spoke of the birds as his "chickens," and the Duncans followed his example.

The very next Sabbath, Duncan, with his wife and children, followed Freckles to the swamp. They saw a sight so wonderful that it kept them talking all the remainder of their lives, and made them unfailing friends of all the birds.

Freckles' "chickens" were awaiting him at the edge of the clearing. They cut the frosty air round his head into curves and circles of crimson, blue, and black.

They chased one another from Freckles, and swept so closely themselves that they brushed him with their outspread wings.

At their feeding-ground, Freckles set down his old pail of scraps and swept the snow from a small level space with a broom improvised of twigs. As soon as his back was turned, the birds clustered over the food, snatching scraps to carry to the nearest bushes.

Several of the boldest, a big crow and a couple of jays, settled on the rim and feasted at leisure, while a cardinal, which hesitated to venture, fumed and scolded from a twig overhead.

Then Freckles scattered his store. At once the ground resembled the spread mantle of Montezuma, except that this mass of gaily coloured feathers was on the backs of living birds.

While they feasted, Duncan gripped his wife's arm and stared in astonishment; for from the bushes and dry grass, with gentle cheeping and queer, throaty chatter, as if to encourage one another, came flocks of quail.

Without anyone seeing it arrive, a big grey rabbit sat in the midst of the feast, contentedly gnawing a cabbage-leaf.

"Weel, I be drawed on!" came Mrs. Duncan's tense whisper.

"Shu-shu," cautioned Duncan.

Lastly Freckles removed his cap. He began filling it with handfuls of wheat from his pockets. In a swarm the grain-eaters arose round him as a flock of tame pigeons.

They perched on his arms and on the cap, and, in the stress of hunger, forgetting all caution, a brilliant cock cardinal and an equally gaudy jay fought for a perching-place on his head.

"Weel, I'm beat," muttered Duncan, forgetting the silence imposed on his wife. "I'll hae to give in. Seein' is believin'."

Freckles emptied his cap, turned his pockets, and scattered his last grain. Then he waved goodbye to his watching friends and started down the timber-line.

A week later, Duncan and Freckles rose from the breakfast-table to face the bitterest morning of the winter.

When Freckles, warmly capped and gloved, stepped to the corner of the kitchen for his scrappail, he found a big pan of steaming boiled wheat on the top of it. He wheeled to Mrs. Duncan with a shining face.

"Were you fixing this warm food for my 'chickens' or yours?" he asked.

"It's for yours, Freckles," she said. "I was afeared in this cold weather they wadna lay good without a warm bite now and then."

Duncan laughed as he stepped to the other room for his pipe; but Freckles faced Mrs. Duncan with a trace of every pang of starved mother-hunger he ever had suffered written large on his homely, splotched, narrow features.

"Oh, how I wish you were my mother!" he cried.

Mrs. Duncan attempted an echo of her husband's laugh.

"Lord love the lad!" she exclaimed. "Bless ye, laddie, I am your mother!"

She tucked the coarse scarf she had knit for him closer over his chest and pulled his cap lower over his ears, but Freckles, whipping it off and holding it under his arm, caught her rough, reddened hand and pressed it to his lips in a long kiss.

Then he hurried away to hide the happy, embarrassing tears that were coming straight from his swelling heart.

Chapter
Two

So Freckles fared through the bitter winter. He was very happy. He had hungered for freedom, love, and appreciation so long!

He had been unspeakably lonely at the Home; and the utter loneliness of a great desert or forest is not as difficult to endure as the loneliness of being constantly surrounded by crowds of people who do not care in the least whether one is living or dead.

All through the winter Freckles' entire energy was given to keeping up his lines and preventing his "chickens" from freezing or starving.

When the first breath of spring touched the Limberlost, and the snow receded before it, and when the catkins began to bloom and there came a hint of green to the trees, bushes, and swale, something new stirred in the breast of the boy.

He never had been so well. Clean, hot, and steady the blood pulsed in his veins. He was always hungry, and his most difficult work tired him not at all. For long months he had tramped those seven miles of trail twice each day, through every conceivable state of weather.

With the heavy club he gave his wires a sure test, and between sections, first in play, afterwards to keep his circulation going, he acquired the skill of an expert drum-major.

Now the Limberlost did not contain last year's terrors. He had made excursions into the interior until he was familiar with every path and road that ever had been made.

As flock after flock of the birds returned and he recognised the old echoes reawakening, he found to his surprise that he had been lonely for them and hailed their return with great joy.

Yet he was filled with a vast impatience and a longing that he scarcely could endure.

It was June by the zodiac, June by the Limberlost, and, with every delight of a newly resurrected season, it should have been June in the hearts of all men. Yet Freckles scowled darkly as he came down the trail.

He was bending the rank grass with his cudgel, and thinking of the shade the denser swamp afforded, when he suddenly dodged sideways; the cudgel whistled sharply through the air and Freckles sprang back.

From the clear sky above him, first level with his face, then skimming, dipping, tilting, whirling until it struck, quill down, in the path in front of him, came a glossy, iridescent, big black feather.

Freckles picked it up and turned the big quill questioningly, and his awed eyes swept the sky.

'A feather dropped from Heaven!' he thought reverently. 'Are the Holy Angels moulting? But no; if they were, it would be white.

'Maybe some poor Black Angel is so tired of being punished that it's standing at the Gates, beating its wings trying to make the Master hear!'

Again and again Freckles searched the sky, but there was no answering gleam of golden gates, no sign of a bird sailing across; then he went slowly on his way, turning the feather and wondering about it.

It was a wing quill, eighteen inches in length, with a heavy spine, grey at the base, shading to jet-black at the tip, and it caught the play of the sun's rays in slanting gleams of green and bronze.

Before him spread a large green pool filled with rotting logs and leaves and bordered with delicate ferns and grasses, among which lifted the creamy spikes of the arrowheads, the blue of the water-hyacinths, and the delicate yellow of the jewel-flowers.

As Freckles leaned over, handling the feather and staring first at it and then into the depths of the pool, he gave voice to his query:

"I wonder what it is!"

Straight across from him, couched in the mosses covering a soggy old log, a big green bull-frog, with palpitant throat and batting eyes, lifted his head and bellowed in answer:

"Fin' dout! Fin' dout! Find out!"

Freckles had the answer. Something seemed to snap in his brain. There was a wavering flame before his eyes. Then his mind cleared. His head lifted in a new poise, his shoulders squared, and his spine straightened.

The agony was over. His soul floated free. Freckles had learned what he sought.

"Before God, I will!"

He uttered the oath so impressively that the "recording angel" never winced as he posted it in the prayer-column.

Freckles set his hat over the top of one of the locust posts used between trees to hold up the wire and fastened the feather securely in the band.

He took out his pencil and account-book, and on a back page he figured that he had walked the timber-line ten months.

His pay was thirty dollars a month and his board cost him eight, which left twenty-two dollars a month, and the two dollars were more than his clothing had cost him.

At the very least he had two hundred dollars in the bank. He drew a deep breath of satisfaction and smiled at the sky with heavenly sweetness.

"I'll be having a book about all the birds, trees, flowers, butterflies, and—yes, by gummy! I'll be having one about the frogs too—if it takes every cent I have," he promised himself.

He put away the account-book that was his most cherished possession, caught up his stick, and started down the line.

The even tap-tap and the cheery, gladsome whistle carried far ahead of him the message that Freckles was himself again.

He fell into a rapid pace, for he had lost time that morning, and as he rounded the last curve he was almost running. There was just a chance that the Boss might be there for his weekly report.

Then, wavering, flickering, darting here and

there over the sweet marsh-grass, came a large
black shadow, sweeping so closely before him
that for the second time that morning Freckles
dodged and sprang back.

He had seen some owls and hawks of the
swamp that he thought could be classed as large
birds, but never anything like this; its big, shining
wings spread six feet.

Its strong feet could be seen drawn among
its feathers, and the sun glinted on its sharp,
hooked beak. Its eyes glowed, caught the light,
and seemed able to pierce the ground at his
feet.

It cared no more for Freckles than if he
had not been there. It perched on a low tree,
and a second later awkwardly hopped to the
trunk of a lightning-riven elm, turned its back,
and sent an eye searching the blue.

Freckles looked just in time to see a second
shadow sweep the grass; another bird, a trifle
smaller and not quite so brilliant in the light,
slowly sailed down and perched beside the
first.

Evidently they were mates, for with a queer,
rolling hop the first-comer shivered his bronze
wings, sidled to the new arrival, and gave her a
sly little peck on her wing.

Then he coquettishly drew away and ogled
her. He lifted his head and waddled a few steps
from her, awkwardly ambled back, and gave her
such a simple sort of kiss on her beak that Freckles
burst into a laugh, then clapped his hand over
his mouth to stifle the sound.

The lover ducked and side-stepped a few
feet, he spread his wings, and slowly and softly

waved them precisely as if he were fanning his
charmer.

Then a wave of uncontrollable tenderness
struck him, and he hobbled to his bombardment
once more.

He faced her squarely this time, and turned
his head from side to side with queer little jerks
and indiscriminate peckings at her wings and
head.

She yawned and shuffled away indifferent-
ly.

Freckles reached up, pulled the quill from
his hat, and, looking from it to the birds, nodded
in settled conviction.

"So you're my Black Angels, you spalpeens!
No wonder you didn't get in! But I'll back you to
come closer to it than any other birds ever did.
You fly higher than I can see.

"Have you picked the Limberlost for a good
place and come to try it? Well, you can be my
'chickens' too, if you want to!"

Freckles broke into an unrestrained laugh,
for the lover-bird was keen about his courting,
and evidently his mate was diffident.

When he approached too boisterously, she
relieved him of a goodly tuft of feathers and sent
him backwards in a series of squirmy little jumps
that gave the boy an idea of what had happened
up-sky to send the falling feather across his path-
way.

"Score one for the lady! I'll be umpiring
this," volunteered Freckles.

With a ravishing swagger, half-lifted wings,
and deep, guttural hissing, the lover came on
again. Suddenly he lifted his body, but she coolly

rocked forward on the limb, glided gracefully beneath him, and slowly sailed into the Limberlost.

Freckles hurried down the trail, shaking with laughter. When he neared the path to the clearing and saw the Boss sitting motionlessly on the mare that was the pride of his heart, the boy broke into a run.

"Oh, Mr. McLean!" he cried. "I hope I haven't kept you waiting very long! And the sun is getting hot! I have been so slow this morning!

"I could have gone faster," he added, "only there were that many things to keep me, and I didn't know you would be here. I'll hurry, after this.

"I've never had to be giving excuses before. The line wasn't down, and there wasn't a sign of trouble; it was other things that were making me late."

McLean, smiling at the boy, immediately noticed the difference in him. This flushed, panting, talkative lad was not the same creature who had sought him in despair and bitterness.

He watched in wonder as Freckles mopped the sweat from his forehead, and he began to laugh.

Then, forgetting all his customary reserve with the Boss, the pent-up boyishness in Freckles broke forth. With an eloquence of which he never had dreamed, he told his story.

He talked with such enthusiasm that McLean never took his eyes from the boy's face or shifted in the saddle until Freckles described the strange lover-bird, and then the Boss suddenly bent over the pommel and laughed with him.

Freckles decorated his story with keen appreciation and rare touches of Irish wit and drollery that made it most interesting as well as very funny. It was a first attempt at descriptive narration.

McLean laughed. "Your story of the big black birds sounds like genuine black vultures. They are common enough in the south, but I never before heard of any this far north.

"You have described perfectly our nearest equivalent to a branch of these birds called in Europe 'Pharaoh's Chickens,' but if they are coming to the Limberlost they will have to drop 'Pharaoh' and become 'Freckles' Chickens,' like the remainder of the birds. Unless they are too odd and ugly to interest you?"

"Oh, not at all, at all!" cried Freckles, bursting into pure brogue in his haste. "I don't know as I'd be calling them exactly pretty, and they do move like a loping rocking-horse, but they are so big and fearless.

"And fly? Why, just think, Sir, they must be flying miles straight up, for they were out of sight completely when the feather fell, and then—"

Freckles' voice trailed off and he hesitated.

"Then what?" urged McLean interestedly.

"He was loving her so," answered Freckles in a hushed voice. "I know it looked awful funny, and I laughed, but if I'd taken time to think, I don't believe I'd have done it. I've seen such little loving in my life."

There was retrospection in his eyes as he continued:

"At the Home it was always the old story of neglect and desertion. People didn't even care enough for their children to keep them, so you see, Sir, I had to like him for trying so hard to make her know how he loved her.

"Of course, they're only birds, but if they are caring for each other like that, why, it's just the same as people, ain't it?"

Freckles lifted his brave, steady eyes to the Boss.

"If anybody loved me like that, Mr. McLean, I wouldn't be spending any time on how they looked or moved. All I'd be thinking of was how they felt towards me."

His voice had a little throb in it.

"If they will stay, I'll be caring as much for them as any 'chickens' I have. Even if I did laugh at him, I thought he was just fine!"

The face of McLean was a study; but the honest eyes of the boy were so compelling that he found himself answering:

"You are right, Freckles. He's a gentleman, isn't he? And the only real chicken you have. Of course he'll remain! The Limberlost will be Paradise for his family.

"And now, Freckles, what has been the trouble all spring? You have done your work as faithfully as anyone could ask, but I can't help seeing that there is something wrong. Are you tired of your job?"

"I love it," answered Freckles. "It will almost break my heart when the gang comes and begins tearing up the swamp and scaring away my 'chickens.'"

"Then what is the matter?" insisted McLean.

"I think, Sir, it's been books," answered

Freckles. "You see, I didn't realise it myself until the bullfrog told me this morning.

"I hadn't ever heard about a place like this. So, being among these beautiful things every day, I got so anxious to know and to name them that it ate into me and made me near sick."

He sighed.

"Of course, I learned to read, write, and figure some at school, but there was nothing there, or in any of the City that I ever got to see, that would make a fellow even be dreaming of such interesting things as there are here.

"I've seen the Parks—but good Lord, they ain't even beginning to be in it with the Limberlost! It's all new and strange to me. I don't know a thing about any of it!"

His voice was awed as he finished:

"The bullfrog told me to 'find out,' plain as day, and books are the only way; ain't they?"

"Of course," said McLean, astonished at himself for his heartfelt relief.

He had not guessed until that minute what it would have meant to him to have Freckles give up.

"You know enough to study out what you want yourself, if you have the books, don't you?"

"I am pretty sure I do," said Freckles. "I learned all I'd the chance to at the Home, and my schooling was good so far as it went.

"It will be all I'll want if I can have some books and learn the real names of things, where they come from, and why they do such interesting things.

"It's been fretting me more than I knew to be shut up here among all these wonders and not know a thing. I wanted to ask you what some books would cost me, and if you'd be having the goodness to get me the right ones. I think I have enough money."

Freckles handed up his account-book and the Boss studied it gravely.

"You needn't touch your bank-account, Freckles," he said. "Ten dollars from this month's pay will get you everything you need to start on. I will write a friend in Grand Rapids today and ask him to select the very best for you and send them at once."

Freckles' eyes were shining.

"I never owned a book in my life!" he said. "Even my school-books were never mine. Lord! How I used to wish I could have just one of them for my very own! How long will it be taking, Sir?"

"Ten days should do it nicely," said McLean. Then, seeing Freckles' lengthening face, he added:

"I'll have Duncan get you a ten-bushel store-case the next time he goes to town. He can haul it to the west entrance and set it up wherever you want it. You can spend your spare time filling it with the specimens you pick up until the books come, and then you can study what you have.

"I suspect you could find a lot of stuff that I could send to naturalists in the City and sell for you. I'll order you a butterfly-net and specimen-box and show you how scientists pin specimens. Possibly you can make a fine collection of these swamp beauties.

"It will be all right for you to take unusual types of moths and butterflies, but I don't want to hear of you killing any birds. They are protected by heavy fines."

McLean rode away and left Freckles staring, aghast. Then he saw the point and smiled. Standing on the trail, he twirled the feather and thought over the morning.

"Well, if life ain't getting to be worth living!" he said wonderingly. "Biggest streak of luck I ever had! About time something was coming my way, but I wouldn't ever have thought anybody could strike such magnificent prospects through just a falling feather."

*   *   *

On Duncan's return from his next trip to town there was a big store-case loaded on the back of his waggon.

He drove to the west entrance to the swamp, set the case on a stump that Freckles had selected in a beautiful, sheltered place, and made it secure on its foundation with a tree at its back.

Duncan next made a door from the lid of the case and fastened it with hinges. Then he drove a staple, screwed on a latch, and gave Freckles a small padlock—so that he might fasten in his treasures safely.

He made a shelf at the top for the books, and last of all he covered the case with oil-cloth.

It was the first time in Freckles' life that anyone ever had done that much for his pleasure, and it warmed his heart with pure joy.

If the interior of the case already had been filled with the rarest treasures of the Limberlost he could not have been happier.

When the big head-teamster stood back to look at his work, he laughingly said:

" 'Neat, but not gaudy,' as McLean says. All we're needing now is a coat of paint to make a cupboard—that would turn Sarah green with envy. Ye'll find that safe an' dry, lad, an' that's all that's needed."

"Mr. McLean sent you?" asked Freckles, his eyes wide and bright with happiness. "It's so good of him. How I wish I could do something that would please him as much!"

"Why, Freckles," said Duncan, as he knelt and began collecting his tools, "I canna see that it will hurt ye to be told that ye are doin' every day a thing that pleases the Boss as much as anything ye could do.

"Ye're being uncommon faithful, lad, and honest as old Father Time. McLean is trusting ye as he would his own flesh and blood."

"Oh, Duncan!" cried the happy boy. "Are you sure?"

"Why, I know," answered Duncan. "Else I wadna venture to say so. In those first days he cautioned me na to tell ye, but now he wadna care. D'ye ken, Freckles, that some of the single trees ye are guarding are worth a thousand dollars?"

Freckles caught his breath and stood speechless. He appeared limp, and he stared straight ahead.

"Ye see," said Duncan, "that's why they must be watched so closely. They take, say, for instance, a burl maple—by sawin' it thin that way, they get finish for thousands of dollars' worth of furniture from a single tree.

"If ye dinna watch faithful, and Black Jack gets out a few he has marked, it means the loss of more money than ye ever dreamed of, lad.

"The other night, down at camp, some son of Balaam was suggestin' that ye might be sellin' the Boss out to Jack and lettin' him take the trees secretly, and nobody wad ever ken till the gang gets here."

A wave of scarlet flooded Freckles' face and he blazed hotly at the insult.

"And the Boss," continued Duncan, coolly ignoring Freckles' anger, "he lays back just as cool as cowcumbers an' says, 'I'll give a thousand dollars to any man that will show me a fresh stump when we reach the Limberlost,' Some of the men just snapped him up that they'd find some. So you see how the Boss is trustin' ye, lad?"

"I am gladder than I can ever express," said Freckles. "And now I will be walking double-time to keep some of them from cutting a tree to get all that money."

Freckles picked up his club and started down the line, whistling cheerily, and he had an unusually long repertoire upon which to draw.

Duncan went straight to the Lower Camp and, calling McLean aside, repeated the conversation verbatim, ending:

"And nae matter what happens now or ever, dinna ye dare let anythin' make ye believe that Freckles hasna guarded faithful as any man could."

"I don't think anything could shake my faith in that lad," answered McLean.

Freckles was whistling merrily. He kept one eye religiously on the line. The other he divided between the path, his friends of the wire, and a search of the sky for his latest arrivals.

Every day since their coming he had seen them, either hanging as small, black clouds above the swamp or bobbing over logs and trees with their queer, tilting walk.

Whenever he could spare time, he entered the swamp and tried to make friends with them, and they were the tamest of all his countless subjects.

They ducked, dodged, and ambled round him, over logs and bushes, and not even a near approach would drive them to flight.

For two weeks he had found them circling over the Limberlost regularly, but one morning the female was missing and only the big black "chicken" hung sentinel above the swamp.

His mate did not reappear during the following days, and Freckles grew very anxious.

He spoke of it to Mrs. Duncan, and she quieted his fears by raising a delightful hope in their stead.

"Why, Freckles, if it's the hen-bird ye are missing, it's ten to one she's safe," she said. "She's laid and is setting, ye silly! Watch him and mark whaur he lights. Then follow and find the nest. Some Sabbath we'll all go an' see it."

Accepting this theory, Freckles began searching for the nest. Because these "chickens" were large, as the hawks, he looked among the tree-tops until he almost sprained the back of his neck. He already had half the crow- and hawk-nests in the swamp located, and he devoted all his spare time to searching for this particular nest, instead of collecting specimens for his store-case.

He found the pair, in the middle of one fore-noon, on the elm where he had watched their love-making. The big black "chicken" was feeding his mate.

So it was proved that they were a pair, they both were alive, and undoubtedly she was brood-ing.

Late that afternoon, coming from a long day on the trail, Freckles saw Duncan's children awaiting him much closer to the swale than they usually ventured, and from their wild gestures he knew that something had happened.

He began to run, but the cry that reached him was:

"The books have come!"

How they hurried! Freckles lifted the young-est to his shoulder, the second took his club and dinner-pail, and when they came up they found Mrs. Duncan at work on a big box.

Lifting the lid, they removed the packing and found that in the box were books on birds, trees, flowers, moths, and butterflies. There was also one about bullfrogs, true to life, as Freckles had hoped.

Besides these were a butterfly-net, a natural-ist's tin specimen-box, a bottle of cyanide, a box of cotton, a paper of long, steel specimen-pins, and a letter telling what all these things were and how to use them.

At the discovery of each treasure Freckles shouted:

"Will you be looking at this, now!"

*   *   *

When Freckles started for the trail the next morning the shining new specimen-box flashed

on his back. The black "chicken," a mere speck
in the blue, caught the gleam of it and wondered
what it was.

The folded net hung beside the boy's hatchet and the bird-book was in the box.

He walked the line and tested each section
scrupulously, watching every foot of the trail, for
he was determined not to slight his work; but if
ever a boy "made haste slowly" in a hurry, it was
Freckles that morning.

When at last he reached the space which he
had cleared and planted round his store-case, his
heart swelled with the pride of possessing so
much that he could call his own, and his quick
eyes feasted on the beauty of it.

He had made a large room, with the door of
the case set even with one side of it. On three
sides, fine big bushes of wild rose climbed to the
lower branches of the trees. His walls were part
mallow, and part alder, thorn, willow, and dog-
wood.

Below, there filled in a solid mass of pale
pink sheep-laurel and yellow St. John's wort,
while the amber threads of the dodder interlaced
everywhere. At one side the swamp came close
and cattails grew in profusion.

In front of them he had planted a row of
water-hyacinths without disturbing in the least
the state of their azure bloom, and, where the
ground rose higher for his floor, a row of foxfire,
which soon would blossom.

To the left he had discovered a queer, natural arrangement of the trees, where they grew to
giant size and were set in a gradually narrowing
space so that a long, open vista stretched away
until lost in the dim recesses of the swamp.

A little trimming of underbrush, rolling of dead logs, levelling of floor, and carpeting of moss made it easy to understand why Freckles had named this the "Cathedral"; yet he never had been taught that "the groves were God's first temples."

On either side of the trees, which constituted the first arch of this dim vista of the swamp, he had planted ferns that grew waist-high this early in the season, and so skilfully had the work been done that not a frond drooped.

Opposite, he had cleared a space for a flower-bed, and had filled one end with every delicate, lacy vine and fern that he could transplant successfully. The body of the bed was a riot of colour, and every day saw the addition of new specimens. The place would have driven a botanist wild.

On the line side he had left the bushes thick for concealment, and he entered by a narrow path which he and Duncan had cleared while setting up the case. He called this the front door, although he used every precaution to hide it.

He had built rustic seats between several of the trees, levelled the floor, and thickly carpeted it with rank, heavy, woolly-dog moss.

Round the case he had planted wild clematis and bitter-sweet and wild grape-vines, and had trained them over it until it was almost covered.

Every day he planted new flowers, cut back rough bushes, and coaxed out graceful new blossoms. His pride in his room was very great, but he had no idea how surprisingly beautiful it would appear to anyone who had not witnessed its growth and construction.

This morning Freckles walked straight to his

case, unlocked it, and set his apparatus and dinner inside.

He planted close to the trail a new specimen he had found, and, bringing his old scrap-bucket from the corner in which it was hidden, from a nearby pool he dipped water and poured it over his carpet and flowers.

Then he took out the bird-book, settled comfortably on a bench, and with a deep sigh of satisfaction turned to the section headed "V." Past "veery" and "vireo" he went, down the line, until his finger, trembling with eagerness, stopped at "vulture," and he read aloud:

" *'Great black California vulture.'*

"Humph! This side of the Rockies will do for us.

" *'Common turkey-buzzard.'*

"Well, we ain't hunting common turkeys. McLean said 'chickens,' and what he says goes.

" *'Black vulture of the South.'*

"Here we are, arrived at once."

Freckles' finger followed the line as he read scraps:

" *'Common in the South. Sometimes called Jim Crow. Nearest equivalent to C-a-t-h-a-r-t-e-s A-t-r-a-t-a.'*

"How the devil am I ever to learn them corkin' big words by myself?

" *'The Pharaoh's Chickens, of European species. Sometimes stray north as far as Virginia and Kentucky . . .'*

"And sometimes farther," interpolated Freckles, " 'cause I got them right here in Indiana, so much like these pictures that I can just see my big 'chicken' bobbing up to get his ears boxed. Hey—

" 'Light-blue eggs. . .'

"Golly! I got to be seeing them!"

" '. . .Big as a common turkey's, but shaped like a hen's, heavily splotched with chocolate—'

"Caramels, I suppose. And—"

" '. . .In hollow logs or stumps.'

"Oh, hagginy! Wasn't I barking up the wrong tree, though? Ought to have been looking close to the ground all this time."

Freckles put away his book, dampened the smudge-fire, without which the mosquitoes made the swamp almost unbearable, gathered up his cudgel and lunch, and went to the line.

At dinner-time he sat on a log and ate and drank his last drop of water. The heat of June was growing intense. Even on the west side of the swamp, where one had full benefit of the breeze from the upland, it was beginning to be unpleasant in the middle of the day.

He brushed the crumbs from his knees and sat resting a little and watching the sky to see if his big "chicken" was hanging up there.

But he came back to the earth abruptly, for there were steps coming down the trail that were neither McLean's nor Duncan's—and there never had been others.

Freckles' heart leaped hotly. He ran a quick hand over his belt to feel if his revolver and hatchet were there, caught up his cudgel and laid it across his knees—and then sat quietly, waiting.

Was it Black Jack, or someone even worse?

Forced to do something to brace his nerves, he puckered his stiffening lips and began whistling the tune which he had led in his clear tenor every year of his life at the Home Christmas exercises:

*"Who comes this way, so blithe and gay,
Upon a merry Christmas day?"*

His quick Irish wit roused to the ridiculous-
ness of it and he burst into a laugh that steadied
him amazingly.

Through the bushes he caught a glimpse of
the oncoming figure. His heart flooded with joy,
for it was a man from the gang.

Wessner had been his bunk-mate the night
he first came down the trail. He knew him as
well as he knew any other of McLean's men. This
was no timber-thief. No doubt the Boss had sent
him with a message. Freckles sprang up and
called cheerily, a warm welcome on his face.

"Well, it's good telling if you're glad to see
me," said Wessner, with something like relief.
"We been hearing down at the camp that you
were so mighty touchy you didn't allow a man
within a rod of the line."

"Nor do I," answered Freckles, "if he's a
stranger; but you're from McLean, ain't you?"

"Oh, damn McLean!" said Wessner.

Freckles gripped the cudgel until his knuck-
les slowly turned purple.

"Are you really saying so?" he enquired with
elaborate politeness.

"Yes, I am," said Wessner. "So would every
man of the gang, if they wasn't too big cowards
to say anything, except maybe that other slob-
bering old Scotsman, Duncan.

"Grinding the lives out of us! Working us
like dogs, and paying us starvation wages, while
he rolls up his millions and lives like a Prince!"

Green lights began to play through Freckles'
grey eyes.

"Wessner," he said impressively, "you'd make a fine pattern for the father of liars! Every man on that gang is strong and healthy, paid all he earns, and treated with the courtesy of a gentleman! As for the Boss living like a Prince, he shares fare with you every day of your lives!"

Wessner was not a born diplomat, but he saw that he was on the wrong tack, so he tried another.

"How would you like to make a good big pile of money without even lifting your hand?" he asked.

"Humph!" said Freckles. "Have you been up to Chicago and cornered wheat, and are you offering me a friendly tip on the investment of my fortune?"

Wessner came close.

"Freckles, old fellow," he said, "if you let me give you a pointer, I can put you on to making a cool five hundred without stepping out of your tracks."

Freckles drew back.

"You needn't be afraid of speaking up," he said. "There isn't a soul in the Limberlost save the birds and the beasts, unless some of your sort's come along and is crowding the privileges of the legal tinints."

"None of *my* friends along," said Wessner. "Nobody knew I came but Black Ja—I mean, a friend of mine. If you want to hear sense and act with reason, he can see you later, but it ain't necessary. We can make all the plans needed. The trick's so dead small and easy."

"Must be, if you have the engineering of it," said Freckles. But he had heard, with a sigh of relief, that they were alone.

Wessner was impervious.

"You just bet it is! Why, only think, Freckles, slavin' away at a measly little thirty dollars a month, and here is a chance to clear five hundred in a day! You surely won't be the fool to miss it!"

"And how was you proposing for me to get it?" enquired Freckles. "Or am I just to find it laying in my path beside the line?"

"That's it, Freckles," blustered the Dutchman, "you're just to find it. You needn't do a thing. You needn't know a thing.

"You name a morning when you will walk up the west side of the swamp and then turn round and walk back down the same side again, and the money is yours. Couldn't anything be easier than that, could it?"

"Depends entirely on the man," said Freckles.

The lilt of a lark hanging above the swale beside them was not sweeter than the sweetness of his voice.

"To some it would seem to come easy as breathing; and to some, wringing the last drop of their hearts' blood couldn't force them!

"I'm not the man that goes into a scheme like that with the blindfold over my eyes, for, you see, it means to break trust with the Boss; and I've served him faithful as I knew how. You'll have to be making the thing very clear to my understanding."

"It's dead easy," repeated Wessner. "You see, there's a few trees in the swamp that's real gold-mines. There's three especial. Two are back in, but one's square on the line. Why, your pottering old Scot fool of a Boss nailed the wire to it with

his own hands! He never noticed where the bark
had been peeled, or saw what it was."

His voice was scornful as he went on:

"Now, if you will stay on this side of the
trail just one day, we can have it cut, loaded,
and ready to drive out at night. Next morning
you can find it, report, and be the busiest man in
the search for us. We know where to fix it all
safe and easy."

He laughed.

"Then McLean has a bet up with a couple of
the gang that there can't be a raw stump found
in the Limberlost. There's plenty of witnesses to
swear to it, and I know three that will.

"There's a cool thousand, and this tree is
worth all of that, raw. Say, it's a gold-mine I tell
you, and just five hundred of it is yours. There's
no danger on earth to you, for you've got McLean
so bamboozled that you could sell out the whole
swamp and he'd never mistrust you. What do you
say?"

Freckles' soul was satisfied.

"Is that all?" he asked.

"No, it ain't," said Wessner. "If you really
want to brace up and be a man and go into the
thing for keeps, you can make five times that in a
week. My friend knows a dozen others we could
get out in a few days, and all you'd have to do
would be to keep out of sight.

"Then you could take your money and skip
some night, and begin life like a gentleman somewhere else. What do you think about it?"

Freckles purred like a kitten.

" 'Twould be a rare joke on the Boss," he
said, "to be stealing from him the very thing he's
trusted me to guard, and be getting my wages

all winter throwed in free. And you're making the pay awful high. Me to be getting five hundred for such a simple little thing as that! You're treating me most Royal indeed!

"It's way beyond all I'd be expecting. Seventeen cents would be a big price for that job. It must be looked into thorough.

"Just you wait here until I do a minute's turn in the swamp, and then I'll be escorting you out to the clearing and giving you the answer."

Freckles lifted the overhanging bushes and hurried to his store-case. He unslung the specimen-box and laid it inside with his hatchet and revolver. Then he slipped the key into his pocket and went back to Wessner.

"Now for the answer," he said. "Stand up!"

There was iron in his voice and he was as commanding as an outraged General.

"Anything you want to be taking off?" he questioned.

Wessner showed the astonishment he felt.

"Why, no, Freckles," he said.

"Have the goodness to be calling me Mr. McLean," snapped Freckles. "I'm reservin' my pet name for the use of my friends!

"Now, you may stand with your back to the light or be taking any advantage you want."

"Why, what do you mean?" sputtered Wessner.

"I'm meaning," said Freckles tersely, "to lick a quarter-section of hell out of you, and may the Holy Virgin stay me before I leave you here as carrion, for your carcass would turn the stummicks of my 'chickens'!"

At the camp that morning, Wessner's conduct had been so palpable an excuse to force a

discharge that Duncan moved near McLean and
whispered:

"Think of the boy, Sir?"

McLean was so troubled that, an hour later,
he mounted Nellie and followed Wessner to the
swamp and silently crept close just in time to
hear Wessner whine:

"But I can't fight you, Freckles. I hain't done
nothing to you. I'm way bigger than you, and
you've only one hand."

The Boss slid off his coat and crouched
among the bushes, ready to spring; but as Freckles' voice reached him he held himself, with the
effort of his life, to learn what mettle was in the
boy.

"Don't you be wasting my good time in the
numbering of my hands," howled Freckles. "The
strength of my cause will make up for my weak-
ness, and the size of a cowardly thief doesn't
count. You'll think all the wild-cats of the Limberlost are turned loose on you when I come agin
you.

"The Boss was for taking me up," he went
on, "washing, clothing, and feeding me, and giving me a home full of love and tenderness, and a
master to look to, and good, well-earned money
in the bank."

His voice rose as he went on:

"He's trusting me his heartful, and here
comes you, you spotted toad of the big road, and
insults me, an honest Irish gentleman, by hinting
that I'd be willing to shut my eyes while you rob
him of the thing I was set and paid to guard,
and then act the sneak and liar to him, and eternally blacken the soul of me.

"You damned rascall" raved Freckles. "Be

fighting before I forget the laws of a gentleman's game and split your dirty head with my stick!"

Wessner backed away, mumbling:

"But I don't want to hurt you, Freckles!"

"Oh, don't you!" raged the boy, now fairly frothing. "Well, I'm itchin' like death to git my fingers in the face of you."

He danced up and, as Wessner lunged in self-defence, ducked under his arm as a bantam and punched him in the pit of the stomach so that he doubled with a groan.

Before Wessner could straighten himself, Freckles was on him, fighting like the wildest fury that ever left the beautiful island.

The Dutchman dealt thundering blows that sometimes landed and sent Freckles reeling, and sometimes missed, while he went plunging into the swale with the impetus of them.

Freckles could not strike with half Wessner's force, but he could land three blows to the Dutchman's one.

It was here that Freckles' days of alert watching on the line, the perpetual swinging of the heavy cudgel and the endurance of all weather, stood him in good stead, for he was tough and agile.

He danced, ducked, and dodged. For the first five minutes he endured fearful punishment. Then Wessner's breath commenced to whistle between his teeth, when Freckles had only begun to fight. He sprang back and cried with shrill laughter:

"Begolly! And will your honour be whistling the horn-pipe for me to be dancing of?"

Spang! went his fist into Wessner's face, and he was past him and into the swale.

"And would you be pleased to tune up a little livelier?" he said, gasping, and clipped his ear as he sprang back.

Wessner lunged at him in blind fury.

Freckles, seeing an opening, forgot the laws of a gentleman's game and drove the toe of his heavy wading-boot into Wessner's middle until he doubled and fell heavily.

In a flash Freckles was on him again.

For a time McLean could not see what was happening.

"Go! Go to him now!" he commanded himself, but so intense was his desire to see the boy win alone that he could not stir.

At last Freckles sprang up and backed away. "Will you get up and be facing me?"

As Wessner struggled to his feet, he resembled a battlefield, for his clothing was in ribbons and his face and hands were streaming blood.

"I—guess I got enough," he mumbled.

"Oh, do you?" roared Freckles. "Well, this ain't your say. You come onto my ground, lying about my Boss and intimatin' I'd steal from his very pockets.

"Now, will you be standing up and taking your medicine like a man, or getting it poured down the throat of you like a baby? I ain't had enough! This is only just the beginning with me. Be looking out there!"

He sprang against Wessner and sent him rolling. He attacked the unresisting figure and fought him until he lay limp and quiet and Freckles had no strength left even to lift an arm. Then he rose and stepped back, gasping for breath.

With his first lungful of air he shouted

"Time!" But the figure of Wessner remained motionless.

Freckles watched him with a regardful eye and saw at last that he was completely exhausted. He bent over him and, catching him by the back of the neck, jerked him to his knees.

Wessner lifted the face of a whipped cur, and, fearing further punishment, burst into shivering sobs, while the tears washed tiny rivulets through the blood and muck.

Freckles stepped back, glaring at Wessner; but then suddenly the scowl of anger and the ugly disfiguring red faded from the boy's face. He dabbed at a cut on his temple from which issued a tiny crimson stream, and jauntily shook back his hair.

His face took on the innocent look of a cherub, and his voice rivalled that of a brooding dove, but into his eyes crept a look of diabolical mischief.

He glanced vaguely round him until he saw his club, seized and twirled it as a drum-major, stuck it upright in the muck, and marched on tiptoe to Wessner, mechanically, as a puppet worked by a string.

Bending over, Freckles reached an arm round Wessner's waist and helped him to his feet.

"Careful, now," he cautioned. "Be careful, Freddy; there's danger of you hurting me."

Fishing a handkerchief from a back pocket, Freckles tenderly wiped Wessner's eyes and nose.

"Come, Freddy, my child," he admonished Wessner; "it's time little boys were getting home.

I've my work to do, and can't be entertaining
you any more today."

Again an awful wrenching seized McLean.

Freckles stepped back as Wessner, tottering
and reeling as a thoroughly drunken man, went
towards the path, appearing indeed as if wild-cats
had attacked him.

The cudgel spun high in air, and, catching
it with an expertise acquired by long practise on
the line, the boy twirled it a second, bonnily shook
back his thick hair, stepped onto the trail, and
followed Wessner.

Wessner turned and mumbled:

"What you following me for?"

Freckles called the Limberlost to witness.

"How's that for the ingratitude of a beast?
And me, troubling myself to show him off my
territory with the honours of war!"

Then he changed his tone completely and
added:

"Belike it's this, Freddy. You see, the Boss
might come riding down this trail any minute,
and the little mare's so wheedlesome that if she
came on to you in your present state, she might
stop so short that she'd send Mr. McLean out over
the ears of her.

"No disparagement intended to the sense of
the mare!" he added hastily.

Wessner belched as he issued a fearful oath,
and Freckles laughed merrily.

"That's a sample of the thanks for a generous
act," he continued. "Here's me, neglecting my
work to escort you out proper, and you saying
such awful words. Do you want me to soap out
your mouth?

"You don't seem to be realising it, but if you

was to buck into Mr. McLean in your present state, without me there to explain matters, the chance is he'd cut the liver out of you; and I shouldn't think you'd be wanting such a fine gentleman as him to see that it's white!"

Wessner grew ghastly under his grime and broke into a staggering run.

"And now will you be looking at the manners of him?" questioned Freckles plaintively. "Going without even a 'thank you,' right in the face of all the pains I've taken to make it interesting for him!"

Freckles twirled the baton and stood as a soldier at attention until Wessner left the clearing, but it was the last scene of that performance.

When the boy turned, there was a deathly illness on his face, and his legs wavered beneath his weight.

He staggered to the case, opened it, and took out a piece of cloth, which he dipped into the water. Then, sitting on a bench, he wiped the blood and grime from his face, while his breath hissed between his clenched teeth.

Shivering with pain and excitement, he unbuttoned the band of his right sleeve, turned it back, and exposed the blue-lined, calloused whiteness of his maimed arm, now vividly streaked with contusions, while in a series of circular dots the blood oozed slowly.

Here Wessner had succeeded in setting his teeth. When Freckles saw what it was, he forgave himself the kick in the pit of Wessner's stomach, and cursed fervently and deep.

"Freckles—Freckles!" said McLean's voice.

Freckles snatched down his sleeve and rose to his feet.

"Excuse me, Sir," he said. "I thought myself to be alone."

McLean pushed him carefully back onto the seat, and, bending over him, opened a pocket-case that he carried as regularly as his revolver and watch, for cuts and bruises were of daily occurrence among the gang.

Taking the hurt arm, he turned back the sleeve and bathed and bound the wounds. He examined Freckles' head and body and convinced himself that there was no permanent injury, although the cruelty of the punishment the boy had borne set the Boss shuddering.

Then he closed the case, shoved it into his pocket, and sat beside Freckles.

All the indescribable beauty of the place was strong round him, but he saw only the bruised face of the suffering boy, who had hedged for the information he wanted as a diplomat, argued as a judge, fought as a sheik, and triumphed as a devil.

When the pain lessened and breathing relieved Freckles' pounding heart, he watched the Boss from the corner of his eye.

How McLean had gotten there and how long he had been there Freckles did not dare ask.

At last he rose, went to the case, took out his revolver and the wire-mending apparatus, and locked the door. Then he turned to McLean.

"Have you any orders, Sir?" he asked.

"Yes," said McLean, "I have, and you are to follow them to the letter. Turn over that apparatus to me and go straight home. Soak yourself in the hottest bath your skin will bear, then go to bed at once. Now hurry."

"Mr. McLean," said Freckles, "it's sorry I am

to be telling you, but this afternoon's walking of
the line ain't done.

"You see, I was just for getting to my feet to
start, and I was on good time, when up came a
gentleman, and we got into a little heated argu-
ment.

"It's either settled or just begun; but between
us, I'm so late I haven't started for the afternoon
yet. I must be going at once, for there's a tree I
must find before the day's over."

"You plucky little idiot," McLean said with a
growl. "You can't walk the line! I doubt if you
can get to the Duncans'. Don't you know when
you're done up? You go to bed; I'll finish your
work."

"Never!" protested Freckles. "I was just a little knocked out a minute ago. But I'm all right
now. They day's hot and the walk's a good seven
miles, Sir. Never!"

As he reached for his outfit, he pitched forward and his eyes closed. McLean stretched him
out on the moss and applied restoratives.

When Freckles returned to consciousness,
McLean ran to the cabin to fetch Nellie the horse,
and to tell Mrs. Duncan to prepare a hot bath.

That worthy woman promptly filled the
wash-boiler and set a roaring fire under it, then
pushed the horse-trough from its base and rolled
it into the kitchen.

By the time McLean returned, leading Nellie,
who had Freckles on her back, Mrs. Duncan was
ready. She and the Boss laid Freckles in the
trough and poured on hot water until he
squirmed.

They soaked, rubbed, and scoured him. Then
they let off the hot water and closed his pores

with cold. Lastly they stretched him on the floor and chafed, rubbed, and kneaded him until he cried out for mercy.

As they rolled him into bed, his eyes dropped shut, but a little later they flared open.

"Mr. McLean!" he cried. "The tree! Oh, do be looking after the tree!"

McLean bent over him.

"Which tree, Freckles?"

"I don't know exact, Sir; but it's on the East Line, and the wire is fastened to it. He bragged that you nailed it yourself, Sir. You'll know it by the bark having been laid open to the grain somewhere low down. And it was five hundred dollars he offered me—to be—selling you out!"

Freckles' head rolled over and his eyes dropped shut again. McLean towered above him. The boy's bright hair waved on the pillow.

His face was swollen and purple with bruises. His left arm, with the hand battered almost out of shape, stretched beside him, and the right, with no hand at all, lay across a chest that was a mass of purple welts.

McLean's mind travelled to the night, almost a year before, when he had engaged Freckles, a stranger.

"Bless the gritty little devil," McLean said with a growl.

Then he went out and told Mrs. Duncan to keep close watch on Freckles, and to send Mr. Duncan to him at the swamp the minute he came home.

Following the trail to the line and back to the scene of the fight, the Boss entered Freckles' study softly, as if his spirit, sleeping there, might

be roused, and gazed round with astonished
eyes.

How had the boy conceived it? What a picture he had wrought in living colours! He had
the heart of a painter. He had the soul of a poet.

The Boss stepped carefully on the velvety
carpet and touched the walls of crisp verdure
with gentle fingers. He stood long beside the
flower-bed, and gazed at the banked wall of
bright blooms as if he doubted its reality.

Where had Freckles ever found such ferns,
and how had he transplanted them?

Here was evidence of a heart aching for
beauty, art, companionship, and worship. It was
written large all over the floor, walls, and furnishings of that little Limberlost clearing.

When Duncan came, McLean told him the
story of the fight, and they laughed until they
cried. Then they started round the line in search
of the tree.

"Now the boy is in for trouble!" said Duncan.

"I hope not," answered McLean. "You never
in all your life saw a cur whipped so completely.
He won't come back for the repetition of the
chorus.

"We surely can find the tree. But if we can't,
Freckles can. I will bring enough of the gang to
take it out at once. That will ensure peace for a
time, at least, and I am hoping that in a month
more the whole gang can be moved here.

"It soon will be fall, and then, if he will go, I
intend to send Freckles to my mother to be educated. With his quickness of mind and body and
a few years' good help, he can do anything.

"Why, Duncan, I'd give a hundred-dollar bill if you could have been here and seen for yourself."

"Yes, and I'd-a done murder," muttered the big teamster. "I hope, Sir, ye'll make good your plans for Freckles, though I'd as soon see any born child o' my own taken from our home. We love the lad, me and Sarah."

Locating the tree was easy, because it was so well identified.

When the rumble of big lumber-waggons passing the cabin on the way to the swamp awakened Freckles the next morning, he sprang up and was soon following them.

He was so sore and stiff that every movement was torture at first, but it grew easier, and shortly he did not suffer so much.

McLean scolded him for coming, yet in his heart he triumphed over every new evidence of fineness in the boy.

The tree was a giant maple, and so precious that they almost dug it out by the roots. When it was down, cut in lengths, and loaded, there was yet an empty waggon.

As they were gathering up their tools to go, Duncan said:

"There's a big hollow tree somewhere mighty close here that I've been wanting for a watering-trough for my stock; the one I have is so small.

"The Portland company cut this for elm butts last year, and it's six feet diameter and hollow for forty feet. It was a buster! While the men are here and there is an empty waggon, why mightn't I load it on and take it up to the barn as we pass?"

McLean said he was very willing, ordered

the driver to pull break line and get the log, and detailed men with the loading-apparatus to assist.

He had told Freckles to ride with him on a section of the maple, but now the boy asked to enter the swamp with Duncan.

"I don't see why you want to go," said McLean. "I have no business to let you out today at all."

"It's my 'chickens,'" whispered Freckles in distress. "You see, I was just after finding yesterday, from my new book, how they do be nesting in hollow trees, and there ain't too many in the swamp. There's just a chance that they might be in that one."

"Go ahead," said McLean. "That's a different story. If they happen to be there, why, tell Duncan he must give up the tree until they have finished with it."

Then he climbed onto a waggon and was driven away.

Freckles hurried into the swamp. He was some little distance behind, yet he could see the men. Before he overtook them, they had turned from the west road and had entered the swamp towards the east.

They stopped at the trunk of a monstrous prostrate log. It had been cut close, three feet from the ground, over three-fourths of the way through, and had fallen to the east, the body of the log still resting on the stump.

The underbrush was almost impenetrable, but Duncan plunged in and with a crowbar began tapping along the trunk to decide how far it was hollow, so that they would know where to cut.

As they awaited his decision, there came from the mouth of it, on wing, a large black bird that swept over their heads.

Freckles danced wildly. "It's my 'chickens'! Oh, it's my 'chickens'!" he shouted. "Oh, Duncan, come quick! You've found the nest of my precious 'chickens'!"

Duncan hurried to the mouth of the log, but Freckles was before him. He crashed through poison vines and underbrush regardless of any danger, and climbed up on the stump.

When Duncan came he was shouting like a wild thing.

"It's hatched!" he yelled. "Oh, my big 'chicken' has hatched out a little 'chicken,' and there's another egg. I can see it plain, and oh, the funny little white baby! Oh, Duncan, can you see my little white 'chicken'?"

Duncan could easily see it, and so could everyone else. Freckles crept into the log and tenderly carried the hissing, blinking little thing to the light in a leaf-lined hat.

The men found it sufficiently wonderful to satisfy even Freckles, who had forgotten that he had ever been sore or stiff, and coddled over it with every blarneying term of endearment he knew.

Duncan gathered his tools.

"Deal's off, boys!" he said cheerfully. "This log canna be touched until Freckles' chickies have finished with it. We might as weel go, gang. Better put it back, Freckles. It's just out, and it may chill. Ye will probably have two in the morn."

Freckles crept back into the log and carefully deposited the baby beside the egg. When he came back he said:

"I made a big mistake not to be bringing the egg out with the baby, but I was fearing to touch it.

"It's shaped like a hen's egg, and it's big as a turkey's, and the beautifulest blue—and splattered with big brown splotches, just like my book said. But you never saw such a sight as it made on the yellow of the rotten wood beside that funny leathery-faced little white baby."

"Tell you what, Freckles," said one of the teamsters. "Have you ever heard of this Bird Woman that goes all over the country with a camera and makes pictures?

"She made some on my brother Jim's place last summer, and Jim's so wild about them he quits ploughing and goes after her about every nest he finds. He helps her all he can to get them, and then she gives him a picture.

"Jim's so proud of what he has that he keeps them in the Bible. He shows them to everybody that comes, and brags about how he helped to make them.

"If you're smart, you'll send for her and she'll come and make a picture just like life. If you help her, she will give you one. It would be uncommon pretty to keep, after your birds are gone.

"Well," the teamster added, "I'm going to town. I go right past her place. I've a big notion to stop and tell her. If she drives straight back into the swamp on the west road, and turns east at this big sycamore, she can't miss finding the tree, even if you ain't here to show her."

"Will you be sure to tell her to come?" asked Freckles.

Duncan slept at home that night. He heard

Freckles slipping out early the next morning, but he was too sleepy to wonder why, until he came to do his morning chores.

When he found that none of his stock was at all thirsty, and saw the water-trough brimming, he knew that the boy was trying to make up to him for the loss of the big trough that he had been so anxious to have.

"Bless his fool little hot heart!" said Duncan. "And him so sore it is tearing him to move for anything. Nae wonder he has us all loving him!"

Freckles was moving briskly, and his heart was so happy that he forgot all about the bruises. He hurried round the trail, and on his way down the east side he went to see the "Chickens."

The mother-bird was on the nest. He thought the other egg might be hatching, so he did not venture to disturb her.

He made the round and reached his study early. He had his lunch along, and did not need to start on the second trip until the middle of the afternoon.

The heat became more insistent. Noon came, and Freckles ate his dinner and settled for an hour or two on a bench with a book.

Chapter
Three

Perhaps there was a breath of sound—afterwards Freckles never could remember—but for some reason he lifted his head just as the bushes parted and the face of an Angel looked through them.

Saints, nymphs, and fairies had floated down the aisle of his Cathedral for him many times in his dreams, with forms and voices of exquisite beauty.

But parting the wild roses at the entrance was beauty of which Freckles never had dreamed. Was it real, or would it vanish as the other dreams?

He dropped his book and, rising to his feet, went a step closer, gazing intently.

This was real flesh and blood. It was in every way kin to the Limberlost, for no bird of its branches swung with easier grace than that with which this dainty young thing rocked on the bit of morass where she stood.

A sapling beside her was not straighter or rounder than her slender form. Her soft, waving hair clung round her face, from the heat, and curled over her shoulders. It was all of one piece with the gold of the sun filtering between the branches.

Her eyes were the deepest blue of the iris, her lips the reddest red of the foxfire, and her cheeks exactly of the same satin as the wild-rose petals caressing them. She was smiling at Freckles in perfect confidence.

"Oh, I'm so delighted that I've found you!" she cried.

"Oh—were you looking for me?" he asked, and his voice quavered incredulously.

"I hoped I might find you," said the Angel. "You see, I didn't do as I was told, and I'm lost. The Bird Woman said I should stay in the carriage until she came back. But she's been gone hours. It's a perfect Turkish bath in there, and I'm all lumpy with mosquito-bites.

"Just when I thought that I couldn't bear it another minute, along came the biggest *Papilio Ajax* you ever saw. I knew how pleased she'd be, so I ran after it. It flew so slow and so close to the ground that a dozen times I thought I had it. Then all at once it went from sight above the trees, and I couldn't find my way back!

"I think I've walked more than an hour. I have been mired to my knees, a thorn raked my arm and now it is bleeding, and I'm so tired and warm."

She parted the bushes farther. Freckles saw that her little blue cotton frock clung to her, limp with perspiration. It was torn across the breast, and one sleeve hung open from shoulder to elbow.

Her arm was covered with blood, and gnats and mosquitoes were clustering round it. Her feet were in lace hose and low shoes.

Freckles gasped. In the Limberlost in low shoes! He caught an armful of moss from his carpet and buried it in the ooze in front of her for a footing.

"Get out here so I can see where you are stepping. Quick, for the life of you!" he ordered.

She smiled on him indulgently.

"Why?" she enquired.

"Did anybody let you come here and not be telling you of the snakes?" urged Freckles.

"We met Mr. McLean on the trail, and he did say something about snakes, I believe. The Bird Woman put on leather leggings, and a nice parboiled time she must be having! I've nothing to do but swelter."

"Will you be coming out of there?" Freckles said, groaning.

She laughed as if it were a fine joke.

"Maybe if I'd be telling you I killed a rattler, curled upon that same place you're standing, as long as my body and the thickness of my arm, you'd be moving where I can see your footing," he urged insistently.

"What a perfectly delightful little brogue you speak," she said. "My father is Irish, and half should be enough to entitle me to do that much.

"'Maybe—if I'd—be telling you,'" she imitated, rounding and accenting each word carefully.

Freckles was beginning to feel a wildness in

his head. He had derided Wessner at that same hour two days ago. Now his own eyes were filling with tears.

"If you were understanding the danger!" he continued desperately.

"Oh, I don't think there is much!"

She tilted on the morass.

"If you've killed one snake here, it's probably all there is; and anyway, the Bird Woman says a rattlesnake is a gentleman and always gives warning before he strikes. I don't hear any rattling. Do you?"

"Would you be knowing it if you did?" asked Freckles almost impatiently.

How the laugh of the young thing rippled!

"'Would I be knowing it?'" she mocked. "You should see the swamps of Michigan where they dump rattlers from the marl-dredgers three and four at a time!"

Freckles stood astounded. She did know; and she was not in the least afraid. She was depending on a rattlesnake to live up to his share of the contract and rattle in time for her to move.

The one characteristic an Irishman admires in a woman, above all others, is courage. Freckles worshipped anew. He changed his tactics.

"I'd be more pleased to be receiving you at my front door," he said, "but as you have arrived at the back, will you come in and be seated?"

He waved towards a bench.

The Angel came instantly.

"Oh, how lovely and cool!" she cried.

As she moved across his room, Freckles had difficult work to keep from falling on his knees, for they were very weak, and he was hard-driven by an impulse to worship.

"Did you arrange this?" she asked.

"Yes," said Freckles simply.

"Someone must come with a big canvass and copy each side of it," she said. "I never saw anything so beautiful.

"How I wish I might remain here with you! I will, someday, if you will let me.

"But now, if you can spare the time, will you help me look for the carriage? If the Bird Woman comes back and finds me gone, she will be almost distracted."

"Did you come on the west road?" asked Freckles.

"I think so," she said. "The man who spoke to the Bird Woman said that that was the only place the wires were down. We drove way in, and it was dreadful—over stumps and logs, and we mired to the hubs. I suppose you know, though.

"I should have stayed in the carriage, but I was so tired. I never dreamed of getting lost. I suspect I will be scolded finely. I go with the Bird Woman half the time during the summer vacations.

"I never came within a smell of getting lost before. At first I thought it was going to be horrid; but since I've found you, maybe it will be good fun after all."·

Freckles was amazed to hear himself excusing her.

"It was so hot in there, you couldn't be expected to bear it for hours and not be moving," he said. "I can take you round the trail almost to where you were. Then you can sit in the carriage, and I will go find the Bird Woman."

"You'll be killed if you do! When she stays

this long, it means that she has a focus on something. You see, when she gets a focus, and lies in
the weeds and water for hours, and then someone
comes along and scares her bird away just as she
has it coaxed up—why, she kills them.

"Even if I melt, you mustn't go after her.
She's probably blistered and half eaten up; but
she never will quit until she is satisfied."

"Then it will be safer for me to be taking
care of you," suggested Freckles.

"Now you're talking sense!" said the Angel.

"May I try to help your arm?" he asked.

"Have you any idea how it hurts?" she par-
ried.

"A little," said Freckles.

"Well, Mr. McLean said we'd probably find
his son here—"

"His son!" cried Freckles.

"That's what he said. And that you would
do anything you could for us, and that we could
trust you with our lives. But I would have trusted
you anyway, if I hadn't known a thing about you.
Say, your father is rampaging proud of you, isn't
he?"

"I don't know," answered the dazed Freckles.

"Well, call on me if you want reliable information. He's so proud of you he is all swelled
up like the toad in Aesop's Fables. If you have
ever had an arm hurt like this, and can do anything, why, for pity's sake, do it!"

She turned back her sleeve, holding towards
Freckles an arm of palest cameo, shaped so ex-
quisitely that no sculptor could have chiselled
it.

Freckles unlocked his case, took out some cotton cloth, and tore it in strips. Then he brought a bucket of the cleanest water he could find.

She yielded herself to his touch as a baby, and he bathed away the blood and bandaged the ugly, ragged wound.

He finished by lapping the torn sleeve over the cloth bandage and binding it down with a piece of twine, with the Angel's help about the knots.

Freckles worked with trembling fingers and a face tense with earnestness.

"Is it feeling any better?" he asked.

"Oh, it's well now!" cried the Angel. "It doesn't hurt at all any more."

"I'm mighty glad," said Freckles. "But you had best go and be having your Doctor fix it right, the minute you get home."

"Oh, bother! A little scratch like that!" jeered the Angel. "My blood is perfectly pure. It will heal in three days."

"It's cut cruel deep. It might be making a scar," Freckles said, faltering, his eyes on the ground. " 'Twould—'twould be an awful pity. A Doctor might know of something to be preventing it."

"Why, I never thought of that!" exclaimed the Angel.

"I noticed you didn't," said Freckles softly. "I don't know much about it, but it seems as if most girls would."

The Angel thought intently, while Freckles still knelt beside her. Suddenly she gave herself an impatient little shake and lifted her glorious eyes full to his, and the smile that swept her

sweet young face was the loveliest thing that
Freckles had ever seen.

"Don't let's bother about it," she proposed,
with just the faintest hint of a confiding gesture
towards him. "It won't make a scar. Why, it just
couldn't, when you have dressed it so nicely."

With a shadowy pain in them he lifted his
eyes to hers, and found her expression to be one
of serene, unconscious purity. What she had said
was straight from a kind, untainted young heart.
She had meant every word of it.

Freckles' soul went sick. He scarcely knew
whether he could muster enough strength to
stand.

"We must go and hunt for the carriage," said
the Angel, rising.

In instant alarm for her, Freckles sprang up,
grasped the cudgel, and led the way, sharply
watching every step.

He went as close to the log as he dared, and
with a little searching he found the carriage.

He cleared a path for the Angel and with a
sigh of relief saw her enter it safely.

The heat was intense, and she pushed the
damp hair from her face.

"This is a shame!" said Freckles. "You'll never be coming here again."

"Oh yes I shall!" said the Angel. "The Bird
Woman says that these birds remain over a month
in the nest, and she would like to make a picture
every few days for perhaps seven or eight weeks."

Freckles barely escaped crying aloud for
joy.

"Then don't you ever be torturing yourself
and your horse to be coming in here again," he

said. "I'll show you a way to drive almost to the
nest on the East Trail, and then you can come
round to my room and stay while the Bird Woman works. It's nearly always cool there, and there's
comfortable seats, and water."

"Oh! Did you have drinking-water there?"
she cried. "I was never so thirsty or so hungry in
my life, but I thought I wouldn't mention it."

"And I had not the wit to be seeing!" wailed
Freckles. "I can be getting you a good drink in
no time."

He turned to the trail.

"Please, wait a minute," called the Angel.
"What's your name? I want to think about you
while you are gone."

Freckles lifted his face with the brown rift
across it and smiled quizzically.

"Freckles?" she guessed, with a peal
of laughter. "And mine is—"

"I'm knowing yours," interrupted Freckles.

"I don't believe you do. What is it?" asked
the girl.

"You won't be getting angry?"

"Not until I've had the water, at least."

It was Freckles' turn to laugh. He whipped
off his big, floppy straw-hat, stood uncovered before her, and said, in the sweetest of all the sweet
tones of his voice:

"There's nothing you could be but the
Swamp Angel."

The girl laughed happily.

Once out of her sight, Freckles ran every step
of the way to the cabin, where Mrs. Duncan gave
him a small bucket of water, cool from the well.

He carried it in the crook of his right arm,

and in his left hand he held a basket, filled with bread and butter, cold meat, apple pie, and pickles.

"Pickles are kind-a cooling," Mrs. Duncan had said.

Freckles ran back to the carriage. The Angel was on her knees, reaching for the bucket, as he came up.

"Be drinking slow," he cautioned her.

"Oh!" she cried, with a long breath of satisfaction. "It's so good! You are more than kind to bring it!"

Freckles stood blinking in the dazzling glory of her smile until he scarcely could see to lift the basket.

"Mercy!" she exclaimed. "I think I had better be naming you the 'Angel.' My Guardian Angel."

"Yes," said Freckles. "I look the character every day—but today most emphatically!"

"Angels don't go by looks," replied the girl, laughing.

Then she said in a more serious tone:

"Your father told us you had been scrapping, and he also told us why. I'd gladly wear all your cuts and bruises if I could do anything that would make my father look as peacocky as yours did. He strutted about proper, and I never saw anyone look prouder."

"Did he say he was proud of me?" asked Freckles marvelling.

"He didn't need to," answered the Angel. "He was radiating pride from every pore. Now, have you brought me your dinner?"

"I had my dinner two hours ago," answered Freckles.

"Honest Injun?" bantered the Angel.

"Honest! I brought that on purpose for you."

"Well, if you knew how hungry I am, you would know to the dot how thankful I am," said the Angel.

"Then be eating!" cried the happy Freckles.

The Angel sat beside a big camera, spread the lunch on the carriage-seat, and divided it in halves. She carefully put back into the basket the daintiest parts she could select; the remainder, she ate.

Again Freckles found her to be of the swamp, for though she was almost ravenous, she managed her food as gracefully as his little yellow fellow, and her every movement was easy and charming.

As he watched her with famished eyes, Freckles told her of his birds, flowers, and books, and never realised what he was doing.

He led her horse to a deep pool that he knew of, where the tortured creature drank greedily, and lovingly rubbed him with its nose as he wiped down its welted body with grass.

Suddenly the Angel cried:

"Here comes the Bird Woman!"

Freckles had intended to leave before she came, but now he was glad indeed to be there, for a warmer, more worn, and worse-bitten creature he had never seen.

She was staggering under a load of cameras and paraphernalia. Freckles ran to her aid. He took all he could carry of her load, stowed it in the back of the carriage, and helped her in.

The Angel gave her water, knelt and unfastened her leggings, bathed her face, and offered her some lunch.

Freckles brought the horse. He was not sure about the harness, but the Angel knew, and soon they left the swamp.

Then he showed them how to reach the "chicken" tree from outside the swamp, indicated a cooler place for the horse, and told them how, the next time they came, the Angel could find his room while she waited.

The Bird Woman finished her lunch, then lay back, almost too tired to speak.

"Were you for getting a picture of 'Little Chicken'?" Freckles asked.

"Finely!" she answered. "He posed splendidly. But I couldn't do anything with his mother. She will require coaxing."

"The Lord be praised!" muttered Freckles under his breath.

The Bird Woman began to feel better.

"Why do you call the baby vulture 'Little Chicken'?" she asked, leaning towards Freckles in an interested manner.

" 'Twas Duncan that began it," said Freckles. "You see, through the fierce cold of winter the birds of the swamp were almost starving. It is mighty lonely here, and they were all the company I was having. I got to carrying scraps and grain down to them.

"Duncan was so generous he was giving me of his wheat and corn from his chickens' feed, and he called the birds my 'swamp chickens.'

"Then when these big black fellows came, Mr. McLean said they were our nearest kind to some in the Old World that they called 'Pharaoh's Chickens,' and he called mine 'Freckles' Chickens.' "

"Good enough!" cried the Bird Woman, her splotched-purple face lighting with interest. "You must shoot something for them occasionally, and I'll bring more food when I come.

"If you will help me keep them until I get my series, I'll give you a copy of each study I make, mounted in a book."

Freckles drew a deep breath.

"I'll be doing my very best," he promised, and from the depths of his heart he meant it.

"I wonder if that other egg is going to hatch," mused the Bird Woman. "But I am afraid not. It should have pipped today. Isn't it a beauty! I never before saw either an egg or the young. They are rare this far north."

"So Mr. McLean said," replied Freckles.

Before they drove away, the Bird Woman thanked him for his kindness to her and to the Angel.

She gave him her hand at parting, and Freckles joyfully realised that this was going to be another person for him to love.

After they had driven away, he could not remember whether they even had noticed his missing hand, and for the first time in his life he himself had forgotten it.

When the Bird Woman and the Angel were on the way home, the girl told of the little corner of Paradise into which she had strayed and of her new name.

The Bird Woman looked at the Angel and guessed its appropriateness.

"Did you know Mr. McLean had a son?" asked the Angel. "Isn't the little accent he has, and the way he twists a sentence, too dear? And isn't it too old-fashioned and funny to hear him call his father 'Mister'?"

"It sounds too good to be true," said the Bird Woman, answering the last question first. "There must be something rare about that young man."

She did not find it necessary to tell the Angel that for several years she had known the man who so proudly proclaimed himself Freckles' father to be a bachelor and a Scotsman. The Bird Woman had a fine way of attending strictly to her own business.

Freckles returned to the trail, but he stopped at every wild brier and looked at the pink satiny petals.

She was not of his world, and better than any other he knew it; but she might be his Angel, and he was dreaming of naught but blind, silent worship.

He finished the happiest day of his life, and that night he returned to the swamp as if drawn by an invisible force.

That Wessner would try for his revenge, he knew. That he would be abetted by Black Jack was almost certain. But fear had fled the happy heart of Freckles. He had kept his trust, and he had won the respect of the Boss.

No one ever could wipe from his heart the flood of holy adoration that had welled with the coming of his Angel. He would do his best, and trust for strength to meet the dark day of reckoning that he knew would come sooner or later.

He swung round the trail, briskly tapping the wire, and singing in a voice that could scarcely have been surpassed for sweetness.

At the edge of the clearing he came into the

bright moonlight, and there sat McLean on his
mare. Freckles hurried to him.

"Is there trouble?" he enquired anxiously.

"That's what I wanted to ask you," said the
Boss. "I stopped at the cabin to see you a minute,
before I turned in, and they said you had come
down here. You must not do it, Freckles. The
swamp is none too healthful at any time, and at
night it is rank poison."

Freckles stood combing his fingers through
Nellie's mane, and the dainty creature was twist-
ing her head for his caresses. Then he pushed
back his hat and looked into McLean's face.

"It's come to the 'sleep with one eye open,'
Sir. I'm not looking for anything to be happening
for a week for two, but it's bound to come, and
soon. If I'm to keep my trust as I've promised
you and myself, I've to live here mostly until the
gang comes. You must be knowing that, Sir."

"I'm afraid it's true, Freckles," said McLean.
"And I've decided to double the guard until we
get here. It will be only a few weeks now. But I'm
so anxious for you that you must not be left alone
further. If anything should happen to you, Freckles, it would spoil one of the very dearest plans of
my life."

Freckles heard with dismay the proposition
to place a second guard.

"Oh! No, no, Mr. McLean!" he cried. "Not for
the world! I wouldn't be having a stranger
round, scaring my birds and tramping up my
study, and disturbing all my ways, for any money!

"I am all the guard you need! I will be faithful! I will turn over the lease with no tree missing—on my life, I will! Oh, don't be sending an-

other man to set them saying I turned coward
and asked for help. It will just kill the honour of
my heart if you do it.

"The only thing I want is another gun. If it
really comes to trouble, six cartridges ain't many,
and you know I am slow-like about reloading."

McLean reached into his hip pocket and
handed a big shining revolver to Freckles, who
slipped it beside the one already in his belt.

Then the Boss sat brooding.

"Freckles," he said at last, "we never know
the timber of a man's soul until something cuts
into him deeply and brings the grain out strong.
You've the making of a mighty fine piece of furniture, my boy, and you shall have your own way
these few weeks yet.

"Then, if you will go, I intend to take you to
the City and educate you, and you are to be my
son, my lad—my own son!"

Freckles twisted his fingers in Nellie's mane
to steady himself.

"But why should you be doing that, Sir?" he
asked, his voice faltering.

McLean slid his arm round the boy's shoulders and gathered him close.

"Because I love you, Freckles," he said simply.

Freckles lifted a white face.

"My God, Sir!" he whispered. "Oh, my God!"

McLean tightened his clasp a second longer,
then he rode down the trail.

But to One, above, Freckles knew he must
make acknowledgement for these miracles. His
lips moved and he began talking softly.

"Thank You for each separate good thing

that has come to me," he said, "and above all for
the falling of the feather. For if it didn't really
fall from an Angel, its falling brought an Angel!

"And if it's in the great heart of You to exer-
cise Yourself any further about me—oh, do please
be taking good care of her!"

*   *   *

The following morning, Freckles, inexpres-
sibly happy, circled the Limberlost. He realised
to the fullest the debt that he already owed the
Boss and the magnitude of last night's declaration
and promises.

He was hourly planning to deliver his trust
and then enter with equal zeal on whatever task
his beloved Boss saw fit to set him next.

He wanted to be ready to meet every device
that Wessner and Black Jack could think of to
outwit him. He recognised their double leverage,
for if they succeeded in felling even one tree,
McLean would become liable for his wager.

Freckles' brow wrinkled in his effort to think
deeply and strongly, but from every swaying,
wild rose the Angel beckoned to him.

When he crossed Sleepy Snake Creek and
the goldfinch, waiting as ever, challenged, "See
me?" Freckles saw the dainty, swaying grace of
the Angel instead.

So Freckles dreamed his dreams, made his
plans, and watched his line. He counted not only
the days but the hours of each day.

As he counted them off, every one bringing
her closer, he grew happier in the joy of her coming.

He managed daily to leave some offering at

the big elm log for his black "chickens." He
slipped under the line at every passing, and went
to make sure that nothing was molesting them.

Though it was a long trip, he paid them several extra visits a day for fear that a snake, hawk,
or fox might have found the baby.

For now his "chickens" not only represented
all his former interest in them, they also furnished
the motive that was bringing his Angel.

Possibly he could find other subjects that the
Bird Woman wanted. The teamster had said that
his brother went after her every time he found a
nest.

Well, he never had counted the nests that he
knew of, and it might be that among all the birds
of the swamp some would be rare to her.

The feathered folk of the Limberlost were
practically undisturbed save by their natural enemies. It was very probable that among his
"chickens," others as odd as the big black ones
could be found.

If she wanted pictures of half-grown birds,
he could pick up fifty in one morning's trip round
the line, for he had fed, handled, and made
friends with them ever since their eyes opened.

He had gathered bugs and worms all spring
as he noticed them on the grass and bushes, and
had dropped them into the first little
open mouths he had found. The babies had gladly accepted this queer tri-parent addition to their
natural providers.

When the week was up, Freckles had his
room crisp and glowing with fresh living things
that rivalled every tint of the rainbow, and he
had carried bark and filled all the muckiest
places of the trail.

It was mid-July. The heat of the last few
days had dried the water round and through
the Limberlost, so it was possible to cross it on
foot in almost any direction.

The heat was doing one other thing that was
bound to make Freckles, as a good Irishman,
shiver.

As the swale dried, its inhabitants were seeking the cooler depths of the swamp. They liked
neither the heat nor leaving the field-mice, moles,
and young rabbits of their chosen location.

He saw them crossing the trail every day as
the heat grew intense.

The rattlers were sadly forgetting their manners, for they struck on no provocation whatever,
and did not even remember to rattle afterwards.

Daily Freckles was compelled to drive big
black snakes and blue racers from the nests of
his "chickens."

He saw the Angel when the carriage turned
from the trail into the clearing. They stopped at
the west entrance to the swamp, waiting for him
to precede them down the trail, as he had told
them it was safest for the horse that he should
do so.

They followed the East Line to a point opposite the big "chicken" tree, and Freckles carried in the camera and showed the Bird Woman
a path he had cleared to the log.

He explained to her the effect the heat was
having on the snakes, and then he crept back to
Little Chicken and brought him out to
the light.

As she worked at setting up her camera, he
told her of the birds of the line, and she stared
at him, wide-eyed and incredulous.

They arranged that Freckles should drive the carriage into the east entrance and leave it in the shade, and then take the horse towards the north to a better place he knew.

Then he was to entertain the Angel at his study or on the line until the Bird Woman finished her work and came to them.

"This will take only a little time," she said. "I know where to set the camera now, and Little Chicken is big enough to be good and too small to run away or act very ugly, so I will be coming soon to see about those nests.

"I have ten plates along, and I surely won't use more than two on him, so perhaps I can get some nests or young birds this morning."

Freckles almost flew, for his dream had come true so soon. He was walking the timber-line and the Angel was following him.

He asked to be excused for going first, because he wanted to be sure the trail was safe for her.

He showed her many of the beautiful nests and eggs of the line. She could identify a number of them, but of some she was ignorant.

So they made notes of the number and colour of the eggs, material and construction of the nests, and colour, size, and shape of the birds, and then they went to find them in the book.

At his room, when Freckles lifted the overhanging bushes and stepped back for her to enter, his heart was all out of time and place.

The study was vastly more beautiful than a week previous.

The Angel drew a deep breath and stood gazing first at one side, then at the other, then far down the Cathedral aisle.

"It's just fairy-land!" she cried ecstatically.

Then she turned and stared at Freckles as she had at his handiwork.

"What are you planning to be?" she asked slowly.

"Whatever Mr. McLean wants me to," he replied.

"What do you do most?" she asked.

"Watch my lines."

"I don't mean work!"

"Oh! In my spare time I study in my books."

"Do you work on the room or the books most?"

"On the room just what it takes to keep it up, and the rest of the time on my books."

The Angel eyed him sharply.

"Well, maybe you are going to be a great scholar," she said, "but you don't look it. Your face isn't right for that, but it's got something big in it—something just great.

"I must find out what it is and then you must work on it. Your father is expecting you to do something. One can tell by the way he talks. You should begin right away. You've wasted too much time already."

Poor Freckles hung his head. He never had wasted an hour in his life. There never had been one that was his to waste.

The Angel, studying his face intently, read the thought.

"Oh, I don't mean that!" she cried with the rank dismay of a sixteen-year-old. "Of course you're not lazy! No one ever would think that from your appearance.

"It's this I mean: there is something fine,

strong, and full of power in your face. There is something you are to do in this world, and no matter how you work at all these other things, or how successfully you do them, it is all wasted until you find the *one thing* that you can do best."

Freckles was silent as she went on:

"If you hadn't a thing in the world to keep you, and could do anything you wanted, what would you do?"

"I'd go to Chicago and sing in the First Episcopal Choir," answered Freckles promptly.

The Angel dropped on a seat, and the hat she had removed and held in her fingers rolled to her feet.

"There!" she exclaimed vehemently. "You can see what I'm going to be. Nothing! Absolutely nothing! You can sing? Of course you can sing! It is written all over you."

Clip! Clip! There came the sharply beating hoofs of a swiftly ridden horse down the trail from the north. They both sprang towards the entrance.

"Freckles! Freckles!" called the voice of the Bird Woman.

They were at the trail on the instant.

"Both those revolvers loaded?" she asked.

"Yes," said Freckles.

"Is there a way you can cut across the swamp and get to the 'chicken' tree in a few minutes, and with little noise?"

"Yes."

"Then go flying," said the Bird Woman. "Give the Angel a lift behind me, and we will ride the horse back where you left the carriage and wait for you. I finished Little Chicken and put him back. His mother came so close, I felt sure she would enter the log.

"The light was fine, so I set and focussed the camera and covered it with branches, attached the long hose, and went away over a hundred feet and hid in some bushes to wait.

"A short, stout man and a tall dark one passed me so closely I almost could have reached out and touched them. They carried a big saw on their shoulders. They said they could work until near noon, and then they must lay off until you passed and then try to load and get out at night.

"They went on—not entirely from sight— and began cutting a tree.

"Mr. McLean told me the other day what would probably happen here, and if they fell that tree, he loses his wager on you.

"Keep to the east and north, and hustle. We'll meet you at the carriage. I always am armed, but Babe will need one of your revolvers. We will separate, and creep on them from different sides and give them a fusillade that will send them flying. You hurry, now!"

She lifted the reins and started briskly down the trail. The Angel, hatless and with sparkling eyes, was clinging round her waist.

Freckles wheeled and ran. He worked his way with much care, dodging limbs and bushes with noiseless tread, and cutting as closely to where he thought the men were as he felt he dared if he was to remain unseen.

As he ran he tried to think. It was Wessner, burning for his revenge, and aided by the bully of the locality, that he was going to meet.

He was accustomed to that thought but not to the complication of having two women on his hands who undoubtedly would have to be taken care of, in spite of the Bird Woman's offer to help him.

His heart was jarring as it never had before from running. He must follow the Bird Woman's plan and meet them at the carriage, but if they really did intend to try to help him, he must not allow it.

When he reached the carriage, the Bird Woman and the Angel had hitched the horse and packed the outfit, and were calmly waiting.

The Bird Woman held a revolver in her hand. She wore dark clothing, and they had pinned a big focussing-cloth over the front of the Angel's light dress.

"Give Babe one of your revolvers, quick!" said the Bird Woman. "We will creep up until we are in fair range. The underbrush is so thick and they are so busy that they will never notice us, if we don't make a noise.

"You fire first, then I will pop in from my direction—and then you, Babe, and shoot quite high, or else very low. We mustn't really hit them. We'll go close enough to the cowards to make it interesting, and keep it up until we have them going."

The Bird Woman reached over, and, taking the smaller revolver from his belt, handed it to the Angel.

"Keep your nerve steady, dear; watch where you step, and shoot high," she said. "Go straight at them from where you are. Wait until you hear Freckles' first shot, then follow me as closely as you can, to let them know that we outnumber them.

"If you want to save McLean's wager on you, now you go!" she commanded Freckles, who, with an agonised glance at the Angel, ran towards the east.

The Bird Woman chose the middle distance, and as she moved away, for a last time she cautioned the Angel to lie down and shoot high.

Through the underbrush the Bird Woman crept even more closely than she had intended, found a clear range, and waited for Freckles' shot.

There was one long minute of sickening suspense.

The men straightened for breath. Work was difficult with a hand-saw in the heat of the swamp. As they rested, the big dark fellow took a bottle from his pocket and began oiling the saw.

"We got to keep mighty quiet," he said, "and wait to fell it until that damned guard has gone to his dinner."

Again they bent to their work.

Freckles' revolver spat fire. Lead spanged on steel. The saw-handle flew from Wessner's hand and he reeled from the jar of the shock.

Black Jack straightened, uttering a fearful oath. Then his hat sailed from his head, the shot coming from the far northeast.

The Angel had not waited for the Bird Woman, and her shot scarcely could have been called high.

At almost the same instant, the third shot whistled, from the east. Black Jack sprang into the air with a yell of complete panic, for it ripped a heel from his boot.

Freckles emptied his second chamber, and the earth spattered over Wessner. Shots poured in rapidly.

Without even reaching for a weapon, both men broke for the east road in great leaping bounds, while leaden slugs sang and hissed round them in deadly earnest.

Freckles was trimming his corners as closely as he dared; but the Angel, if she did not really intend to hit, was taking risks in a scandalous manner.

When the men reached the trail, Freckles yelled at the top of his voice:

"Head them off on the south, boys! Fire from south!"

As he had hoped, Black Jack and Wessner instantly plunged into the swale. A spattering of lead followed them. They crossed the swale, running low, with not even one backwards glance, and entered the woods beyond the trail.

Then the little party gathered at the tree.

"I'd better fix this saw so they can't be using it if they come back," said Freckles, taking out his hatchet and making saw-teeth fly.

"Now we must leave here without being seen," said the Bird Woman to the Angel. "It won't do for me to make enemies of these men, for I am likely to meet them while at work any day."

"You can do it by driving straight north on this road," said Freckles. "I will go ahead and cut the wires for you. Don't for your lives ever let it out that you did this, for it's black enemies you would be making."

Freckles clipped the wires and they drove through.

When the Angel leaned from the carriage and held out his revolver, Freckles looked into her face and lost his breath. Her eyes were black and her face was a deeper rose colour than usual. He felt that his own was white as death.

"Did I shoot high enough?" she asked sweetly. "I really forgot about lying down."

Freckles winced. Did the child know how close she had gone? Surely she could not. Or was it possible that she had the nerve and skill to fire like that purposely?

"I will send the first reliable man I meet for McLean," said the Bird Woman, gathering up the reins. "You keep well hidden. There isn't a chance that they will be back, but don't run any risks. Remain under cover."

She laughed as at a fine joke.

"If they should come, it probably would be for their saw."

Round-eyed, Freckles watched the Bird Woman and the Angel drive away.

After they were out of sight and he was safely hidden among the branches of a small tree, he remembered that he had neither thanked them nor said good-bye. Considering what they had been through, they probably never would come again.

He had forgotten the excitement of the morning and the passing of time, when distant voices aroused him and he softly lifted his head.

Nearer and nearer they came, and as the heavy waggons rumbled down the East Trail he could hear them plainly.

The gang were shouting themselves hoarse
for the Limberlost Guard. Freckles did not feel
that he deserved it.

At the sight of Freckles the men threw up
their hats and cheered. McLean shook hands with
him warmly, but big Duncan gathered him into
his arms and hugged him as a bear and choked
over a few words of praise.

The gang drove in and finished felling the
tree. McLean was angry beyond measure at this
attempt on his property, for in their haste to fell
the tree the thieves had cut too high and wasted
a foot and a half of valuable timber.

When the last waggon rolled away, McLean
sat on the stump and Freckles told the story he
was aching to tell. The Boss scarcely could believe his senses. Also, he was greatly disappointed.

"I have been praying almost all the way over,
Freckles," he said, "that you would have some
evidence by which we could arrest those fellows
and get them out of our way, but this will never
do.

"We can't mix up those women in it. They
have helped you save me the tree and my wager
as well. Going across the country as she does, the
Bird Woman never could be expected to testify
against them."

"No, indeed; nor the Angel, Sir," said Freckles.

"The Angel?" queried the astonished Mc-
Lean.

The Boss listened in silence while Freckles
told of the coming and christening of the Angel.

"I know her father well," said McLean at last, "and I have seen her often. You are right, she is a beautiful young girl, and she appears to be utterly free from the least particle of false pride or foolishness. I do not understand why her father risks such a jewel in this place."

"He's daring it because she is a jewel, Sir," said Freckles eagerly. "Why, she's trusting a rattlesnake to rattle before it strikes her, and of course she thinks she can trust mankind as well.

"The man isn't made who wouldn't lay down the life of him for her. But she doesn't need any care. Her face and the pretty ways of her are all the protection she would need in a band of howling savages."

"Did you say she handled one of the revolvers?" asked McLean.

"She scared all the breath out of my body," admitted Freckles. "Seems that her father has taught her to shoot. The Bird Woman told her distinctly to lie low and blaze away high, just to help scare them.

"The spunky little thing followed them right out into the west road, spitting lead like hail, and clipping all round the heads and heels of them; and I'm damned, Sir, if I believe she'd have cared a rap if she'd hit."

"Will they come back?" asked McLean.

"Of course!" said Freckles. "They're not going to be taking that. You could stake your life on it, they'll be coming back. At least Black Jack will.

"Wessner may not have the pluck, unless he's half-drunk. Then he'd be a terror. And the next time—" Freckles hesitated.

"What?"

"It will just be a question of who shoots first and straightest."

"Then the only thing for me to do is to double the guard and bring the gang here the first minute possible," McLean said. "As soon as I feel that we have the rarest of the stuff out below, we will come.

"It won't do to leave you here alone any longer. Black Jack has been shooting twenty years to your one, and it stands to reason that you are no match for him. Who of the gang would you like best to have with you?"

"No one, Sir," said Freckles emphatically. "Next time is where I run. I won't try to fight them alone. I'll just be getting wind of them, and then make tracks for you.

"I'll need to come like lightning, and Duncan has no extra horse, so I'm thinking you'd best get me one—or perhaps a bicycle would be better. It would cost less and be faster than a horse, and would take less care."

As they walked to the cabin, McLean insisted on another guard, but Freckles was stubbornly set on fighting his battle alone.

He made one mental condition! If the Bird Woman was going to give up the "Little Chicken" series, he would yield to the second guard, solely for the sake of her work and the presence of the Angel in the Limberlost.

With McLean it was a case of letting his sober, better judgement be overridden by the boy whom he was growing to love so dearly that he could not endure to oppose him; and to have Freckles keep his trust and win alone meant more than any money the Boss might lose.

The following morning McLean brought the bicycle and Freckles took it to the trail to test it. He went skimming round the trail on it, on a preliminary trip, before he locked it in his store-case and on foot started his minute examination of his line.

He glanced round his room before he left it, and then stood staring.

On the moss before his prettiest seat lay the Angel's hat. In the excitement of yesterday, all of them had forgotten it.

He went and picked it up, oh! so carefully, and gazed at it with hungry eyes, but touching it only to carry it to his case, where he hung it on the shining handlebar of the new bike and locked it among his treasures.

Then he went to the trail, with a new expression on his face and a strange throbbing in his heart. He was not in the least afraid of anything that morning. He felt he was the veriest Daniel, and all his lions seemed weak and harmless.

What Black Jack's next move would be he could not imagine, but that there would be a move of some kind was certain. The big bully was not a man to give up his purpose, nor to have the hat swept from his head by a bullet and bear it meekly.

Moreover, Wessner would cling to his revenge with a Dutchman's singleness of mind.

Freckles tried to think connectedly, but there were too many places on the trail where the Angel's footprints were yet visible.

She had stepped in one mucky spot and left a sharp impression. The afternoon sun had baked it hard, and the horses' hoofs had not obliterated any part of it, as they had in so many places.

Freckles stood, fascinated, gazing at it. He measured it lovingly with his eye. He would not have ventured a caress on her hat any more than on her person, but this was different. Surely a footprint on a trail might belong to anyone who found and wanted it.

He stooped under the wires and entered the swamp. With a little searching, he found a big piece of thick bark loose on a log, and, carefully peeling it, he carried it out and covered the print so that the first rain would not obliterate it.

When he returned to his room, he tenderly laid the hat upon his book-shelf, and, to wear off his awkwardness, mounted his bike and went spinning on the trail again.

It was like flying, for the path had been worn smooth by his feet and baked hard by the sun almost all the way.

When he came to the bark, he veered far to one side and smiled at it in passing.

Suddenly he was off the bicycle, kneeling beside it. He removed his hat, carefully lifted the bark, and gazed lovingly at the imprint.

Deliberately he laid his lips on the footprint. Then he rose, appearing as if he had been drinking at the fountain of gladness.

Chapter
Four

"Do you see anything heavenly about that hat?" queried Freckles, holding it up.

The morning breeze waved the ribbons gracefully, binding one round Freckles' sleeve and the other across his chest, where they caught and clung together as if magnetised.

"Yes," said Sarah Duncan. "It's verra plain and simple, but it juist makes ye feel that it's all of the finest stuff. It's exactly what I'd call a heavenly hat."

"Sure," said Freckles, "for it's belonging to an Angel!"

Then he told her about the hat and asked her what he should do with it.

"Take it to her, of course!" said Sarah Duncan. "Like it's the only she has and she may need it badly."

Freckles smiled. He had a pretty clear idea about the hat being the only one the Angel had. However, there was something which he felt he should do and wanted to do, but he was not sure.

"You think I might be taking it to her home?" he asked.

"Of course ye must," said Mrs. Duncan. "And without another hour's delay. It's been here two days noo, and she may want it, and be too busy or afraid to come."

"But how can I take it?" asked Freckles.

"Go spinning on yer wheel. Ye can do it easy in an hour."

"But in that hour, what if——?"

"Nonsense!" broke in Sarah Duncan. "Ye've watched that timber-line until ye've grown fast to it, lad. Give me your boots and club and I'll walk the south end and watch doon the east and west sides until ye get back."

"Mrs. Duncan! You never would be doing it!" cried Freckles.

"Why not?" she enquired.

"But you know you're mortal afraid of snakes and a lot of other things in the swamp."

"I am afraid of snakes," said Mrs. Duncan, "but likely they've gone into the swamp, this hot weather. I'll juist stay on the trail and watch, and ye might hurry the least bit. Ye go on and take the blessed little Angel her beautiful hat."

"Are you sure it will be all right?" urged Freckles. "Do you think if Mr. McLean came he would care?"

"Na," said Mrs. Duncan, "I dinna."

Freckles knew what he had to do, but there was no use in taking time to try to explain it to Mrs. Duncan while he was so hurried. He exchanged his wading-boots for shoes, gave her his club, and went spinning towards town.

Freckles knew very well where the Angel

lived. He had seen her home many times, and he passed it now without even taking his eyes from the street, steering straight for her father's place of business.

After he had glanced over his bicycle to see that it was all right, and just as he walked to the kerb to remount, he heard a voice that thrilled him through and through, calling:

"Freckles! Oh, Freckles!"

The Angel separated from a group of laughing sweet-faced girls and came hurrying to him. She was in snowy white—a quaint little frock with a marvel of soft lace round her throat and wrists.

Through the sheer sleeves of it her beautiful, rounded arms showed distinctly, and it was cut just to the base of her perfect neck.

On her head was a pure white creation of fancy braid, with folds upon folds of tulle, soft and silken as cobwebs, lining the brim; and a mass of white roses clustered against the gold of her hair, crept round the crown, and fell in a riot to her shoulders at the back.

There were gleams of gold with settings of blue on her fingers, and altogether she was the daintiest, sweetest sight he ever had seen.

Freckles, standing on the kerb, forgot himself, in his cotton shirt, his corduroys, and his belt, from which his wire-cutter and pliers were hanging, and gazed as a man gazes when first he sees the woman he adores with all her charms enhanced by appropriate and beautiful clothing.

"Oh, Freckles!" she cried as she came to him. "I was wondering about you the other day. Do you know, I never saw you in town before. You watch that old line so closely! Why did you come? Is there any trouble? Are you just starting for the Limberlost?"

"I came to bring your hat," said Freckles. "You forgot it in the rush the other day. I have just left it with your father, and a message trying to express the gratitude of me for how you and the Bird Woman were for helping me out."

The Angel nodded gravely, and Freckles saw that he had done the proper thing in going to her father.

Then his heart bounded until it jarred his body, for she was saying that she scarcely could wait for the time to come for the next picture in the "Little Chicken" series.

Freckles stood on the kerb with drooped eyes, for he felt that if he lifted them, the tumult of tender adoration in them would show, and would frighten her.

"I was afraid your experience the other day would scare you so that you'd never be coming again," he found himself saying.

The Angel laughed gaily.

"Did I looked scared?" she questioned.

"No," said Freckles, "you did not."

"Did those men come back?"

"No," said Freckles. "The gang got there a little after noon and took out the tree, but I must tell you, and you must tell the Bird Woman, that there's no doubt but they will be coming back, and they will have to make it before long now, for it's soon the gang will be there to work on the swamp."

"Oh, what a shame!" cried the Angel. "They'll clear out roads, cut down the beautiful

trees, and tear up everything. They'll drive away
the birds and spoil the Cathedral.

"When they have done their worst, then all
the mills close to here will follow in and take out
the cheap timber. Then the landowners will dig
a few ditches and build some fires, and in two
summers more the Limberlost will be full of corn
and potatoes."

They looked at each other and groaned despairingly in unison.

"You like it too," said Freckles.

"Yes," said the Angel. "I love it. Your room is
a little piece right out of the heart of fairy-land,
and the Cathedral is God's work, not yours.

"You only found it and opened the door after
He had completed it. The birds, flowers, and vines
are all so lovely.

"The Bird Woman says it is really a fact that
the mallows, the foxfires, the irises, and the lilies
are larger and of richer colouring there than in
the remainder of the country.

"She says it's because of the rich loam and
muck. I hate seeing the swamp torn up, and to
you it will be like losing your best friend; won't
it?"

"Something like," said Freckles. "Still, I've
the Limberlost in my heart, so that all of it will
be real to me while I live, no matter what they
do to it.

"I'll be glad past telling if you will be coming
a few more times, at least until the gang arrives.
Past that time, I don't allow myself to be thinking."

"Come, have a cool drink before you start
back," said the Angel.

"I couldn't possibly," said Freckles. "I left

Mrs. Duncan on the trail, and she's terribly afraid of a lot of things. If she even sees a big snake I don't know what she'll do."

"It won't take but a minute, and you can ride fast enough to make up for it," pleaded the Angel. "Please. I want to do something fine for you, to make up a little for what you did for me that first day."

Freckles looked in sheer wonderment into the beautiful face of the Angel. Did she truly mean it? Would she walk down that street with him, crippled, homely, in mean clothing, with the tools of his occupation on him, and share with him the treat she was offering?

He could not believe it even of the Angel.

Still, in justice to the candour of her pure, sweet face, he would not think that she would make the offer if she did not mean it.

She really did mean just what she said, but Freckles knew that when it came to carrying out her offer and she saw the stares of her friends and the sneers of her enemies—if such as she could have enemies—and heard the whispered jeers of the curious, then she would see her mistake and be sorry.

It would be only a manly thing for him to think this out, and save her from the results of her own blessed bigness of heart.

"I really must be off," said Freckles earnestly, "but I'm thanking you more than you'll ever know for your kindness. All my way home, in my thoughts I'll just be sipping bowls of some icy drink."

Down came the Angel's foot, and her eyes flashed indignantly.

"There's no sense in that," she said. "When

you knew I was warm and thirsty and you went and brought me a drink, how do you think you would have felt if I wouldn't take it because ... because goodness knows why!

"You can ride faster to make up for the time. I've just thought out what I want to fix for you."

She stepped to his side and deliberately slipped her hand under his arm—his right arm, which ended in an empty sleeve.

"You are coming," she said firmly. "I won't have it any other way."

Freckles could not have told how he felt, nor could anyone else. His blood rioted and his head swam, but he kept his wits.

Bending over her, he said softly:

"Please don't, Angel. You don't understand."

How Freckles himself came to understand was a problem.

"It's this," he persisted. "If your father met me on the street, in my station and dress, with you on my arm, he'd have every right to be caning me before the people, and not a finger would I lift to stay him."

The Angel's eyes snapped.

"If you think my father cares about my doing anything that is right and kind, and that makes me happy to do—why then, you completely failed in reading my father, and I'll ask him and just show you."

She dropped Freckles' arm and turned towards the entrance to the building.

"Why, look there!" she exclaimed.

Her father stood in a big window fronting the street, a bundle of papers in his hand, in-

terestedly watching the little scene with eyes that
comprehended quite as thoroughly as if he had
heard every word.

The Angel caught his glance and made a
despairing little gesture towards Freckles. The
Man of Affairs answered her with a look of infinite
tenderness.

He nodded his head and waved the papers in
the direction she had indicated, and even the
veriest dolt could have read the words his lips
formed:

"Take him along!"

A sudden trembling seized Freckles. At the
sight of the Angel's father he had stepped back
as far from her as he could, and snatched off his
hat.

The Angel turned on him with triumphant
eyes.

She was highly strung and not accustomed
to being thwarted.

"Did you see that?" she demanded. "Now
are you satisfied? Will you come, or must I call
a policeman to bring you?"

Freckles went. There was nothing else to
do.

Wheeling his bicycle, he walked down the
street beside her. On every hand she was kept
busy giving and receiving the cheeriest greet-
ings.

She walked into the parlour exactly as if she
owned it, and a clerk came hurrying to meet
her.

"There's a vacant table beside a window
where it is cool. I'll save it for you."

"Please do not," said the Angel. "I've taken
this man unawares, and he's in a rush. I'm afraid

if we sit down we'll take too much time and afterwards he will blame me."

She walked to the fountain, and a long row of people stared with all the varying degrees of insolence and curiosity that Freckles had felt they would.

He glanced at the Angel. *Now* would she see?

"On my soul!" he muttered under his breath. "They don't even touch her!"

She laid down her sunshade and gloves, then walked to the end of the counter and turned the full battery of her eyes on the attendant.

"Please," she said.

The white-aproned individual stepped back and gave delighted assent. The Angel stepped beside him, and, selecting a tall, flaring glass which was almost paper-thin, she stooped and rolled it in a tray of cracked ice.

"I want to mix a drink for my friend," she said. "He has a long, hot ride before him, and I don't want him started off with one of those old palate-teasing sweetnesses that you mix just on purpose to drive a man back in ten minutes."

There was an appreciative laugh from the line of people at the counter.

"I want a clear, cool, sparkling drink that has a tang of acid in it. Where's the cherry phosphate? That would be good, don't you think?"

The attendant did think. He pointed out the different taps, and the Angel mixed the drink, while Freckles, standing so erect that he almost leaned backwards, gazed at her and paid no attention to anyone else.

When she had the glass brimming, she tilted

a little of its contents into a second glass and tasted it.

"That's entirely too sweet for a thirsty man," she said.

She poured out half the mixture, added a new ingredient, refilled the glass, and tasted it a second time.

Submitting the result to the attendant, she asked:

"Isn't that about the thing?"

He replied enthusiastically:

"I'd get my wages raised ten a month if I could learn that trick."

The Angel carried the brimming, frosty glass to Freckles. He removed his hat, and lifting the icy liquid even with her eyes and looking straight into them, he said in the mellowest of all the mellow tones of his voice:

"I'll be drinking it to the Swamp Angel."

As he had said to her that first day, she now cautioned him:

"Be drinking slowly."

On the street the Angel walked beside Freckles to the first crossing and there she stopped.

"Now, will you promise to ride fast enough to make up for the five minutes that took?" she asked. "I am a little uneasy about Mrs. Duncan."

Freckles wheeled his bicycle into the street. It seemed to him as if he had poured that delicious, icy liquid into every vein in his body instead of his stomach. It even had gone to his brain.

"Did you insist on fixing that drink because you knew how intoxicating 'twould be?" he asked.

There was subtlety in the compliment and it delighted the Angel. She laughed gleefully.

"Next time maybe you won't take so much coaxing," she teased.

"I wouldn't have this time, if I had known your father and been understanding you better.

"Do you really think the Bird Woman will be coming again?"

The Angel laughed again. "Wild horses couldn't drag her away," she cried. "She will have hard work to wait the week out. I shouldn't be in the least surprised to see her start at any hour."

Freckles could not endure the suspense; the question had to come.

"And you?" he asked, but he dared not raise his eyes to hers.

"Wild horses," she said, laughing, "couldn't keep me away either! I dearly love to come, and the next time I am going to bring my banjo, and I'll play; and you'll sing for me some of the songs I like best, won't you?"

"Yes," said Freckles, because it was all he was capable of saying just then.

"It's beginning to act stormy," she said. "If you hurry you will just about make it. Good-bye now."

* * *

Freckles was halfway to the Limberlost when he dismounted. He could ride no farther because he could not see the road.

As he sat under a tree and leaned against it, sobs shook, twisted, and rent him.

If the Angel and the Bird Woman would remind him of his position, speak condescendingly, or notice his hand, he could endure it, but this—it surely would kill him!

His hot, pulsing Irish blood was stirred deeply. What did they mean? Why did they do it? Were they like that to everyone? Was it pity?

It could not be, for he knew that the Bird Woman and the Angel's father must know that he was not really McLean's son, and it did not matter to them in the least. In spite of accident and poverty, they evidently expected him to do something worthwhile in the world.

That must be his remedy. He must work on his education. He must get away. He must find and do the great thing of which the Angel had talked.

For the first time, his thoughts turned anxiously towards the City and the beginning of his studies. McLean and the Duncans spoke of him as "the boy," but he was a man, and he must face life bravely and act a man's part.

The Angel was a mere child. He must not allow her to torture him past endurance with her frank comradeship that to him meant high Heaven, earth's richness, and all that lay between, and to her meant nothing.

There was an ominous growl of thunder, and, amazed at himself, Freckles snatched up his bicycle and raced for the swamp.

He was worried to find his boots lying at the cabin door; the children playing on the wood-pile told him that "Mither" had said they were so heavy she couldn't walk in them, and she had come back and taken them off.

Thoroughly frightened, he stopped only long enough to slip them on, then sped with all his strength for the Limberlost.

To the west, the long, black, hard-beaten trail lay clear; but far up the east side, straight across the path, he could see what was certainly a limp, brown figure.

Freckles spun with all his might.

Sarah Duncan lay face down across the trail. When Freckles turned her over, his blood chilled at the look of horror settled on her face.

There was a low humming and something went *spat!* against him. Glancing round, Freckles shivered in terror, for there was a swarm of wild bees settled on a scrub-thorn only a few yards away.

The air was thick with excited, unsettled bees making ready to go farther in search of a suitable location.

Then he thought he understood, and with a prayer of thankfulness in his heart that she had escaped, even so narrowly, he caught her up and hurried down the trail until they were well out of danger.

He laid her in the shade, and, carrying water from the swamp in the crown of his hat, he bathed her face and hands; but she lay in unbroken stillness, without a sign of life.

She had found Freckles' boots so large and heavy that she had gone back and taken them off, although she was mortally afraid to approach the swamp without them. The thought of it made her nervous, and the fact that she never had been there alone added to her fears.

She had not followed the trail many rods when her trouble had begun. She was not Freckles, and not a bird of the line was going to be fooled into thinking she was.

They kept whizzing from their nests and unexpected places and darting round her head and feet, with quick whirring sounds, which kept her starting and jumping.

Before Freckles was halfway to town, poor Mrs. Duncan was hysterical, and the Limberlost had neither sung nor performed for her.

But there was trouble brewing. It was quiet and intensely hot, with that stifling stillness that precedes a summer storm, and feathers and fur were tense and nervous. The birds were singing only a few broken snatches, and flying round, seeking places of shelter.

One moment everything seemed devoid of life; the next, there was an unexpected whirr, a buzz and a sharp cry. Then a pandemonium of growling, hissing, snarling, and grunting broke loose.

The swale bent flat before heavy gusts of wind, and the big black "chicken" swept lower and lower above the swamp. Patches of clouds gathered, shutting out the sun and making it very dark, and the next moment were swept away.

Then the sun poured with fierce, burning brightness, and everything was quiet.

It was at the first growl of thunder that Freckles really had noticed the weather, and, putting his own troubles aside resolutely, he raced for the swamp.

Sarah Duncan paused.

"Weel, I wouldna stay in this place for a million a month," she said aloud, and the sound of her voice brought no comfort, for it was so little like she had thought it would be that she glanced hastily round to see if it really was she who had spoken.

Tremblingly she wiped the perspiration from her face with the skirt of her sunbonnet.

"Awfu' hot," she said huskily, panting. "B'lieve there's going to be a big storm. I do hope Freckles will hurry."

Her chin was quivering as a terrified child's. She lifted her bonnet to replace it and brushed against a bush beside her.

Whirr, almost into her face, went a nighthawk, stretched along a limb for its daytime nap.

Mrs. Duncan cried out and sprang down the trail, alighting on a frog that was just hopping across. The horrible croak it gave as she crushed it sickened her. She screamed wildly and jumped to one side.

That carried her into the swale, where the grasses reached almost to her waist. Her horror of snakes returning, she made a flying leap for an old log lying beside the line.

She alighted squarely, but it was so damp and rotten that she sank straight through it to her knees. She caught at the wire as she went down, but she missed it, and raked her wrist across a barb until she tore a bleeding gash.

Her fingers closed convulsively round the next strand of wire. She was too frightened to scream now, and her tongue had stiffened. She clung frantically to the sagging wire and finally managed to grasp it with the other hand.

Now she could reach the top wire, so she drew herself up and found solid footing. She picked up the club that she had dropped, and, leaning heavily on it, she managed to return to the trail.

The wind rose higher, the changes from light to darkness were more abrupt, and the thunder came closer and louder at every peal.

A heron, fishing the nearby pool for Freckles' "find-out" frog, fell into trouble with a muskrat and uttered a rasping note that sent Mrs. Duncan a rod down the line without realising that she had moved.

She stopped and looked round her fearfully. Several bees struck her and were angrily buzzing before she noticed them. Then the humming swelled on all sides.

A convulsive sob shook her, and she ran into the bushes, then into the swale, anywhere to avoid the swarming bees, ducking, dodging, fighting for her very life.

As she ran, straining every muscle, she suddenly became aware that crossing the trail before her was a big, round, black body, with brown markings on its back, like painted geometrical patterns. She tried to stop, but the louder buzzing behind warned her that she dare not.

Gathering her skirts higher, with her hair flying round her face and her eyes almost bursting from their sockets, she ran straight towards it.

The sound of her feet and the humming of the bees alarmed the rattler, and it stopped across the trail, lifting its head above the grasses of the swale and rattling enquiringly—rattling until the bees were outdone.

Straight at it went the panic-striken woman, running wildly and uncontrollably. She took one leap, clearing its body on the path, and then flew ahead as if on winged feet.

The snake, coiled to strike, missed Mrs. Duncan and landed among the bees instead. They settled over and round it, among the grasses, and went threshing towards its den in the deep, willow-fringed low ground.

Completely exhausted, Mrs. Duncan staggered on a few steps farther, fell facing the path, where Freckles found her, and lay quietly.

Freckles worked over her until she drew a long, quivering breath and opened her eyes.

When she saw him bending above her, she closed her eyes tightly, gripped him, and struggled to her feet. He helped her up, and with his arm round her, half-carrying her, they made their way to the clearing.

She clung to him and helped herself with all her remaining strength, but open her eyes she would not, until her children came clustering round her.

Then, brawny, big Scotswoman though she was, she quietly keeled over again. The children added their wailing to Freckles' panic.

This time he was so close to the cabin that he could carry her into the house and lay her on the bed. He sent the oldest boy scudding down the trail for the nearest neighbour, and between them they undressed her and discovered that she had not been bitten.

When they had bathed and bound the bleeding wrist and coaxed her back to consciousness, she lay sobbing and shuddering.

The first intelligent words she said were:

"Freckles, look at that jar on the kitchen-table and see if my yeast is na run over."

Several days passed before she could give

Duncan and Freckles any detailed account of
what had happened to her, and then she could
not do it without crying as the smallest of her
babies.

Freckles was almost heartbroken, and nursed
her as well as any woman could have done; while
big Duncan, with a heart full for them both,
worked early and late to chink every crack of the
cabin and examine every spot close to it that
possibly could harbour a snake.

The effects of her morning on the trail kept
her shivering half the time. She could not rest until she sent for McLean and begged him to save
Freckles from further risk in that place of hor-
rors.

The Boss went to the swamp with his mind
fully made to do so. But Freckles stood and
laughed at him.

"Why, Mr. McLean, don't you let a woman's
nervous-system set you worrying about me," he
said. "It's the height of my glory to fight it out
with the old swamp and all that's in it, or will be
coming to it, and then to turn it over to you, as I
promised you and myself I'd do, Sir.

"You couldn't break my heart quicker than
to be taking it from me now, when I'm just on the
home-stretch. It won't be over three or four weeks
now, and when I've been at it almost the year,
why, what's that to me, Sir?

"You mustn't let a woman get mixed up with
business, for I've always heard about how it's
bringing trouble."

McLean smiled.

"What about that last tree?" he asked.

Freckles blushed and grinned appreciative-
ly.

"Angels and Bird Women don't count in the common run, Sir," he affirmed shamelessly.

McLean sat in the saddle and laughed.

*   *   *

The Bird Woman and the Angel did not seem to count in the common run, for they arrived on time for the third of the series, and found McLean on the line, talking to Freckles.

The Boss was filled with enthusiasm by a marsh article of the Bird Woman's that he had just read. He begged to be allowed to accompany her into the swamp and watch the method by which she secured illustrations in such a location.

The Bird Woman explained to him that it was an easy matter with the subject she then had at hand; and as Little Chicken was too small to be frightened by him, and big enough to be growing troublesome, she was glad for his company.

They went to the "chicken" log together, leaving to the happy Freckles the care of the Angel, who had brought her banjo and a roll of songs that she wanted to hear him sing.

The Bird Woman told them that they might practise in Freckles' room until she finished with Little Chicken, and then she and McLean would come to the concert.

It was almost three hours before they finished and came down the West Trail for their rest and lunch.

McLean walked ahead, keeping sharp watch on the trail and clearing it of fallen limbs from overhanging trees. He sent a big piece of bark flying into the swale, and then stopped short and stared at the trail.

The Bird Woman bent forward. Together they studied that imprint of the Angel's foot. At last their eyes met, the Bird Woman's filled with astonishment, and McLean's humid with pity.

Neither said a word, but they knew.

McLean entered the swale and hunted up the bark. He tenderly replaced it, and the Bird Woman carefully stepped over.

As they reached the bushes at the entrance, the voice of the Angel stopped them, for it was commanding and filled with much impatience.

"Freckles James Ross McLean!" she was saying. "You fill me with dark blue despair! You're singing as if your voice were glass and liable to break at any minute. Why don't you sing as you did a week ago? Answer me that, please."

The heart of poor Freckles almost burst with dull pain and his great love for her. In his desire to fulfil her expectations, he forgot everything else, and when she reached his initial chord he was ready.

He literally burst forth:

> *"Three little leaves of Irish green,*
> *United on one stem,*
> *Love, truth, and valour do they mean,*
> *They form a magic gem."*

The Angel's eyes widened curiously, her lips parted, and a deeper colour swept into her cheeks. She had intended to arouse him, and she had more than succeeded.

She was too young to know that in the effort to arouse men, women frequently kindle fires that they can neither quench nor control.

Freckles was looking over her head and singing that song as it never had been sung before, for her alone; and instead of her helping him, as she had intended, he was carrying her with him on the waves of his voice.

When he struck into the chorus, wide-eyed and panting, she was swaying towards him and playing for dear life to keep up.

> *"Oh, do you love,*
> *Oh, say you love,*
> *You love the shamrock green."*

At the last note, Freckles' voice ceased and his gaze fastened on the Angel's. He had given his best and his all. He fell on his knees and folded his arms across his breast.

The Angel, as if magnetised, walked straight down the aisle to him, and, running her fingers into the crisp masses of his red hair, tilted his head back and laid her lips on his forehead.

Then she stepped back and faced him.

"Good boy!" she said, in a voice that wavered from the throbbing of her shaken heart. "Dear boy! I knew you could do it! I knew it was in you! Freckles, when you go into the world, if you can face a big audience and sing like that, just once, you will be immortal, and anything you want will be yours."

"Anything!" Freckles gasped.

"Anything," said the Angel.

Freckles rose, muttered something, and, catching up his old bucket, plunged into the swamp blindly, on the pretence of bringing water.

The Angel walked slowly across the room, sat on the rustic bench, and, through narrowed lids, intently studied the tip of her shoe.

On the trail, the Bird Woman wheeled to McLean with a dumbfounded look.

"God!" muttered he.

At last the Bird Woman spoke.

"Do you think the Angel knew she did that?" she asked softly.

"No," said McLean, "I do not. But the poor boy knew it. Heaven help him!"

The Bird Woman stared across the gently waving swale.

"I don't see how I am going to blame her," she said at last. "It's so exactly what I would have done myself."

"Say the remainder," McLean demanded hoarsely. "Do him justice."

"He is a born gentleman," conceded the Bird Woman. "He took no advantage. He never even tried to touch her. Whatever that kiss meant to him, he recognised that it was the loving impulse of a child under the stress of strong emotion. He was fine and manly as any man ever could have been."

McLean lifted his hat.

"Thank you," he said simply, and parted the bushes for her to enter Freckles' room.

It was her first visit, and before she left she sent for her cameras and made studies of each side of it and of the Cathedral. She was entranced with the delicate beauty of the place, and her eyes kept following Freckles as if she could not believe that it could be his conception and his work.

That was a happy day.

The Bird Woman had brought a lunch, and they spread it, with Freckles' dinner, on the mossy floor, where they sat, resting and enjoying themselves. But the Angel put her banjo into its case and silently gathered her music, and no one mentioned the concert.

The Bird Woman left McLean and the Angel to clear away the lunch, and with Freckles examined the walls of his room and told him all she knew about his shrubs and flowers.

She analysed a cardinal-flower and showed him what he had wanted to know all summer— why the bees buzzed ineffectually round it while the humming-birds found in it an ever-ready feast.

Some of his specimens were so rare that she was unfamiliar with them, and with the flower-book between them they knelt, studying the different varieties.

She wandered the length of the Cathedral aisle with him, and it was at her suggestion that he lighted his altar with a row of flaming fox-fire.

Later, as Freckles went to the cabin after his long day at the swamp, he saw Little Chicken's mother sweeping to the south and wondered where she was going.

He stepped into the bright, cosy little kitchen, and as he reached into the wash-basin he asked Mrs. Duncan:

"Mother Duncan, do kisses wash off?"

So warm a wave swept her heart that a half-flush mantled her face. She straightened her shoulders and glanced at his hands tenderly.

"Lord, na, Freckles!" she cried. "At least, the ones ye get from people ye love dinna, because they dinna stay on the outside.

"They strike in until they find the centre of your heart, and make their stopping-place there, and nothing can take them from ye—I doubt if even death! Na, lad, ye can be reet sure kisses dinna wash off"

Freckles set down the basin and as he plunged his hot, tired face into the water he muttered:

"I needn't be afraid to be washing, then, for that one struck in."

Chapter Five

Freckles took his lunch and went to the swamp. He walked and watched eagerly. He could find no trace of anything, yet he felt a tense nervousness, as if trouble might be brooding.

He examined every section of the wire, and kept watchful eyes on the grasses of the swale, in an effort to discover if anyone had passed through there; but he could discover no trace of anything to justify his fears.

He tilted his hat-brim to shade his face and looked for his "chickens." They were soaring almost beyond sight in the sky.

"Gee!" he said aloud, as if to them. "If I only had your sharp eyes and convenient location now, I wouldn't need be troubling so."

He reached his room and cautiously scanned the entrance before he stepped in. Then he pushed the bushes apart with his right arm and entered, his left hand on the butt of his favourite revolver.

Instantly he knew that someone had been there.

He stepped to the centre of the room, closely scanning each wall and the floor. He could find no trace of a clue to confirm his belief, yet so intimate was he with the spirit of the place that he knew.

How he knew he could not have told, yet he did know that someone had entered his room, sat on his benches, and walked over his floor.

He was most sure round the case. Nothing was disturbed, yet it seemed to Freckles that he could see where prying fingers had tried the lock.

He stepped behind the case, carefully examining the ground all round it, and close beside the tree to which it was nailed he found a deep, fresh footprint in the spongy soil—a long, narrow print that was never made by the foot of Wessner.

His heart tugged in his breast as he mentally measured the print, but he did not linger, for now arose the feeling that he was being watched.

It seemed to him that he could feel the eyes of some intruder at his back. He knew he was examining things too closely: if anyone were watching, he did not want him to know that he felt it.

He took the most open way, and carried water for his flowers and moss as usual; but he put himself into no position in which he was fully exposed, and his hand was close to his revolver constantly.

Growing restive at last under the strain, he plunged boldly into the swamp and searched minutely all round his room, but he could not discover the least thing to give him further cause for alarm.

He unlocked his case, took out his bicycle, and for the remainder of the day he rode and watched as he never had before. Several times he locked the bike and crossed the swamp on foot, zigzagging to cover all the space possible.

Every foot he travelled he used the caution that sprang from knowledge of danger and the direction from which it probably would come.

He thought of sending for McLean, but for his life he could not make up his mind to do it, with nothing more tangible than one footprint to justify him.

He waited until he was sure Duncan would be at home, if he was coming for the night, before he went to supper. The first thing he saw as he crossed the swale was the team of big bays in the yard.

There had been no one passing that day, and Duncan readily agreed to keep watch while Freckles rode to town. He had told Duncan of the footprint, and urged him to guard closely.

Duncan said he might rest easy; then, filling his pipe and taking a good revolver, the big man went to the Limberlost.

Freckles made himself clean and neat, and raced for town, but it was night and the stars were shining before he reached the home of the Bird Woman.

From afar he could see that the house was ablaze with lights. The lawn and verandah were strung with fancy lanterns and alive with people.

He thought his errand important, and to turn back never occurred to Freckles. This was all the time or opportunity he would have. He must see the Bird Woman, and see her now.

He leaned his bicycle inside the fence and walked up the broad front entrance. As he neared the steps he saw that the place was swarming with young people, and the Angel, with an excuse to a group that surrounded her, came hurrying to him.

"Oh, Freckles!" she cried delightedly. "So you could get off? We were so afraid you could not! I'm as glad as I can be!"

"I don't understand," said Freckles. "Were you expecting me?"

"Why, of course!" exclaimed the Angel. "Haven't you come to my party? Didn't you get my invitation? I sent you one."

"By mail?" asked Freckles.

"Yes," said the Angel. "I had to help with the preparations, and I couldn't find time to drive out; but I wrote you a letter, and told you that the Bird Woman was giving a party for me, and we wanted you to come, surely. I told them at the office to put it with Mr. Duncan's mail."

"Then that's likely where it is at present," said Freckles. "Duncan comes to town only once a week, and at times not that. He's home tonight for the first time in a week.

"He's watching an hour for me until I come to the Bird Woman with a bit of work I thought she'd be caring to hear about bad. Is she where I can see her?"

The Angel's face clouded.

"What a disappointment!" she cried. "I did so want all my friends to know you. Can't you stay anyway?"

Freckles glanced from his wading-boots to the patent-leathers of some of the Angel's friends, and smiled whimsically, but there was no danger of his ever misjudging her again.

"You know I cannot, Angel," he said.

"I am afraid I do," she said ruefully. "It's too bad! But there is a thing I want for you more than to come to my party, and that is to hang on and win with your work.

"I think of you every day, and I just pray that those thieves are not getting ahead of you. Oh, Freckles, do watch closely!"

She was so lovely a picture as she stood before him, ardent in his cause, that Freckles could not take his eyes from her to notice what her friends were thinking. If she did not mind, why should he?

Her face and bared neck and arms were like the wild-rose bloom. Her soft frock of white tulle lifted and stirred round her with the gentle evening air.

The beautiful golden hair that crept round her temples and ears as if it loved to cling there was caught back and bound with broad blue satin ribbon. There was a sash of blue at her waist, and knots of it catching up her draperies.

"Must I go after the Bird Woman?" she pleaded.

"Indeed you must," Freckles answered firmly.

The Angel went away, then returned to say that the Bird Woman was telling a story to her guests inside and could not come for a short time.

"You won't come in?" she pleaded.

"I must not," said Freckles. "I am not dressed to be among your friends, and I might be forgetting myself and stay too long."

"Then," said the Angel, "we mustn't go through the house, because it would disturb the story; but I want you to come the outside way to the conservatory and have some of my birthday-lunch and get some cake to take to Mrs. Duncan and the babies. Won't that be fun?"

Freckles thought that it would be more than fun, and he followed delightedly.

The Angel gave him a big glass brimming with some icy, sparkling liquid that struck his palate as it never had been touched before, because a combination of frosty juices had not been a frequent beverage with him.

The night was warm and the Angel was most beautiful and kind. A triple delirium of spirit, mind, and body seized him and he developed a boldness that was all unnatural.

He slightly parted the heavy curtains that separated the conservatory from the company and looked between. He almost stopped breathing. He had read of things like that but he never had seen them.

The open space seemed to stretch through half-a-dozen rooms, all ablaze with lights, perfumed with flowers, and filled with elegantly dressed people. There were glimpses of polished floors, sparkling glass, and fine furnishings. From somewhere, the voice of his beloved Bird Woman arose and fell.

The Angel crowded beside him and was watching also.

"Doesn't it look pretty?" she whispered.

"Do you suppose Heaven is any finer than that?" asked Freckles.

The Angel began to laugh.

"Do you want to be laughing harder than that?" queried Freckles.

"A laugh is always good," said the Angel. "A little more *avoirdupois* won't hurt me. Go ahead."

"Well then," said Freckles, "it's only that I feel all over as if I belong there. I could wear fine clothes, and move over those floors, and hold my own against the best of them."

"But where does my laugh come in?" demanded the Angel, as if she had been defrauded.

"And you ask me where the laugh comes in, looking me in the face after that," marvelled Freckles.

"I wouldn't be so foolish as to laugh at such a manifest truth as that," said the Angel. "Anyone that knows you even half as well as I do knows that you are never guilty of a discourtesy, and you move with twice the grace of any man here. Why shouldn't you feel as if you belong where people are graceful and courteous?"

"On my soul!" said Freckles. "You are kind to be thinking it. You are doubly kind to be saying it."

The curtains parted and a woman come towards them. Her silks and laces trailed across the polished floors. The lights gleamed on her neck and arms, and flashed from rare jewels.

She was smiling brightly, and until she spoke, Freckles had not realised fully that it was his beloved Bird Woman.

Noticing his bewilderment, she cried:

"Why, Freckles! Don't you know me in my war-clothes?"

"I do in the uniform in which you fight the Limberlost," said Freckles.

The Bird Woman laughed.

Then he told her why he had come, and she scarcely could believe him. She could not say exactly when she would go, but she would make it as soon as possible, for she was most anxious to make the study.

As they talked, the Angel was busy packing a box of sandwiches, cake, fruit, and flowers. The Bird Woman gave him a last frosty glass, thanked him repeatedly for bringing news of new material, and then Freckles went into the night.

He rode for the Limberlost with his eyes on the stars. Presently he removed his hat, hung it on his belt, and ruffled his hair to the sweep of the night wind.

He filled the air all the way with snatches of oratorios, gospel-hymns, and dialect and coon songs, in a startlingly varied programme.

The one thing that Freckles knew he could do was sing. The Duncans heard him coming a mile up the trail and could not believe their senses.

Freckles unfastened the box from his belt and gave Mrs. Duncan and the children all the eatables it contained, except one big piece of cake that he carried to the sweets-loving Duncan.

He put the flowers back in the box and set it among his books. He did not say anything, but they understood that it was not to be touched.

"Tha's Freckles' flow'rs," said a tiny Scotsman, "but," he added cheerfully, "it's oor sweet-ies!"

Freckles slowly coloured as he took Duncan's cake and started towards the swamp. While Duncan ate, Freckles told him something about the evening, as well as he could find words to express himself, and the big man was so amazed that he kept forgetting the treat in his hands.

Then Freckles mounted his cycle and began a spin that terminated only when the biggest Plymouth Rock fowl in Duncan's coop saluted a new day and long lines of light reddened the east.

As Freckles rode he sang, and as he sang he worshipped, but the God he tried to glorify was a dim and far-away mystery. The Angel was warm flesh and blood.

Every time he passed the little bark-covered imprint on the trail he dismounted, removed his hat, solemnly knelt, and laid his lips on the impression.

With the near approach of dawn, Freckles sang his last note. Wearied almost to falling, he turned from the trail into the path leading to the cabin for a few hours' rest.

* * *

As Freckles left the trail, from the swale close to the south entrance four large, muscular men rose and swiftly and carefully entered the swamp by the waggon-road. Two of them carried a big saw, the third carried coils of rope and wire, and all of them were heavily armed.

They left one man on guard at the entrance. The other three made their way through the darkness as best they could and were soon at Freckles' room.

He had left the swamp on his bicycle from the West Trail. They counted on his returning on the bike and circling the East Line before he came back to his room.

A little below the west entrance to Freckles' room, Black Jack stepped into the swale, bound a wire tightly round a scrub oak, and carried it below the waving grasses, where he stretched it taut across the trail and fastened it to a tree in the swamp.

Then he obliterated all signs of his work and arranged the grass over the wire until it was so completely covered that only minute examination would reveal it.

They entered Freckles' room with coarse oaths and jests. In a few moments, his specimen-case with its precious contents was rolled into the swamp, and the saw was eating into one of the finest trees of the Limberlost.

The first report from the man they had left on watch was that Duncan had driven to the South Camp; the second was that Freckles was coming. The man watching was sent to see on which side the boy turned in to the path, and, as they had expected, he took the east.

He was a little tired and his head was rather muddled, for he had not been able to sleep as he had hoped, but he was very happy. Although he watched until his eyes ached, he could see no sign of anyone having entered the swamp.

He called a cheery greeting to all his "chickens." At Sleepy Snake Creek he almost fell from his bicycle with surprise, for the sawbill-bird was surrounded by four lanky youngsters clamouring for breakfast. The father was strutting with all the importance of a drum-major.

"No use to expect the Bird Woman today," said Freckles; "but now wouldn't she be jumping for a chance at that?"

As soon as Freckles was far down the East Line, the watch was posted below his room on the west, to report his coming. It was only a few moments before the signal came.

Then the saw stopped and the rope was brought out and uncoiled close to a sapling. Wessner and Black Jack crowded to the very edge of the swamp a little above the wire, and crouched, waiting.

They heard Freckles before they saw him. He came clipping down the line at a good pace, and as he rode he was singing softly:

> "Oh, do you love,
> Oh, say you love—

He got no further. The bicycle struck the tense wire and stopped dead.

Freckles shot over the handlebar and slid down the trail on his chest.

As he struck the ground, Black Jack and Wessner were upon him. Wessner caught off an old felt hat and clapped it over Freckles' mouth, while Black Jack twisted the boy's arm behind him. Then they rushed him to his room.

Almost before he realised that anything had happened, he was trussed to a tree and securely gagged.

Three of the men resumed sawing the tree. The other followed the path Freckles had worn to Little Chicken's tree, and presently reported

that the wires were down and two teams with the
loading-apparatus were coming to take out the
timber.

All the time the saw was slowly eating, eating into the big tree.

Wessner went to the trail and removed the
wire. He picked up Freckles' bicycle and leaned
it against the bushes so that if anyone did pass on
the trail they would not see it lying in the swamp-
grass.

Then he came and stood in front of Freckles
and laughed in devillish hate. To his own amaze-
ment, Freckles found himself looking fear in the
face, and he marvelled that he was not afraid.

Four to one! The tree was halfway eaten
through, the waggons were coming up the inside
road—and he was bound and gagged!

The men with Black Jack and Wessner had
belonged to McLean's gang when last he had
heard of them, but who those coming with the
waggons might be he could not guess.

If they secured that tree, McLean lost its value, lost his wager, and lost his faith in Freckles.

The words of the Angel hammered in his
ears: *"Oh, Freckles, do watch closely!"*

And the saw ate on.

When the tree was down and loaded, what
would they do? Pull out, and leave him there to
report them? It was not to be hoped for. The
place always had been lawless. It could mean
but one thing.

A mist swept before his eyes, and his head
swam. Was it only last night that he had worshipped the Angel in a delirium of happiness?
And now what?

Wessner, released from his turn at the saw, walked to the flower-bed, and tore up a handful of rare ferns by the roots, and started towards Freckles. His intention was obvious. Black Jack stopped him with an oath.

"You see here, Dutchy," he bawled, "mebby you think you'll wash his face with that, but you won't. A contract's a contract. We agreed to take out these trees and leave him for you to dispose of whatever way you please, provided you shut him up eternally on this deal.

"But I'll not see a tied man tormented by a fellow that he can lick up the ground with, loose, and that's flat. It raises my gorge to think what he'll get when we're gone, but you needn't think you're free to begin before. Don't you lay a hand on him while I'm here! What do you say, boys?"

"I say yes," growled one of McLean's latest deserters. "What's more, we're a pack of fools to risk the dirty work of silencing him. You had him face down and were on his back; why the hell didn't you cover his head and roll him into the bushes until we were gone?

"When I went into this, I didn't understand that he was to see all of us and that there was murder on the ticket. I'm not up to it. I don't mind lifting the trees we came for, but I'm cursed if I want blood on my hands."

"Well, you ain't going to get it," bellowed Black Jack. "You fellows only contracted to help me get out my marked trees. He belongs to Wessner, and it ain't our deal what happens to him."

"Yes, and if Wessner finishes him safely, we are practically in for murder as well as stealing the trees; and if he don't, all hell's to pay. I think you've made a damnable bungle of this thing, that's what I think!"

"Then keep your thoughts to yourself," roared Black Jack. "We're doing this, and it's all planned safe and sure. As for killing that buck—come to think of it, killing is what he needs.

"He's way too good for this world of woe anyhow. I tell you, it's all safe enough. His dropping out won't be the only secret the old Limberlost has never told.

"It's too dead easy to make it look like he helped take the timber and then cut. Why, he's played right into our hands. He was here at the swamp all last night, and back again in an hour or so.

"When we get our plan worked out, even old fool Duncan won't lift a finger to look for his carcass. We couldn't have him going in better shape."

"You just bet," said Wessner. "I owe him all he'll get, and be damned to you, but I'll pay!" he said, and snarled at Freckles.

So it was killing, then. They were not only after this one tree, but many, and with his body it was their plan to kill his honour.

To brand him a thief, with them, before the Angel, the Bird Woman, the dear Boss, and the Duncans—Freckles, in sick despair, sagged against the ropes.

Then he gathered his forces and thought swiftly. There was no hope of McLean coming. They had chosen a day when they knew he had a big contract at the South Camp.

The Boss could not come before tomorrow by

any possibility, and there would be no tomorrow for Freckles. Duncan was on his way to the South Camp, and the Bird Woman had said she would come as soon as she could.

However, after the fatigue of the party, it was useless to expect her and the Angel today, and God save them from coming! The Angel's father had said that they would be as safe in the Limberlost as at home. What would he think of this?

The sweat broke on Freckles' forehead. He tugged at the ropes whenever he dared, but they were passed round the tree and his body several times, and knotted on his chest.

He was helpless. There was no hope, no help.

And after they had conspired to make him appear a runaway thief to his loved ones, what was it that Wessner would do to him?

Whatever it was, Freckles lifted his head and resolved that he would bear in mind what he had once heard the Bird Woman say. He would go out bonnily. If he grew afraid, never would he let them see.

After all, what did it matter what they did to his body if by some scheme of the devil they could encompass his disgrace?

Then hope suddenly rose high in Freckles' breast. They could not do that! The Angel would not believe. Neither would McLean. He would keep up his courage. Kill him they could; dishonour him they could not.

Yet, summon all the fortitude he might, that saw eating into the tree rasped on his nerves worse and worse.

With whirling brain he gazed into the Limberlost, searching for something, he knew not what, and in blank horror found his eyes fastened on the Angel.

She was quite a distance away, but he could see her white lips and wide, angry eyes.

"Freckles! Freckles! Oh, Freckles!" called the voice of the Angel. Freckles swayed forward and wrenched at the rope until it cut deeply into his body.

"Hell!" cried Black Jack. "Who is that? Do you know?"

Freckles nodded.

Black Jack whipped out a revolver and snatched the gag from Freckles' mouth.

"Say quick, or it's up with you right now, and whoever that is with you!"

"It's the girl the Bird Woman takes with her," whispered Freckles through dry, swollen lips.

"They ain't due here for five days yet," said Wessner. "We got on to that last week."

"Yes," said Freckles; "but I found a tree covered with butterflies and things along the East Line yesterday that I thought the Bird Woman would want extra, and I went to town for her last night.

"She said she'd come soon, but she didn't say when. They must be here. I take care of the girl while the Bird Woman works.

"Untie me, quick, until she is gone. I'll try to send her back, and then you can go on with your dirty work."

"He ain't lying," volunteered Wessner. "I saw that tree covered with butterflies and him watching round it when we were spying on him yesterday."

"No, he leaves lying to your sort," snapped

Black Jack, as he undid the rope and pitched it across the room.

"Remember that you're covered every move you make, my buck," he cautioned.

"Freckles! Freckles!" came the Angel's impatient voice, closer and closer.

"I must be answering," said Freckles, and Black Jack nodded. "Right here!" he called.

To the men he said: "You go on with your work, and remember one thing yourselves. The work of the Bird Woman is known all over the world. This girl's father is a rich man, and she is all he has.

"If you offer hurt of any kind to either of them, this world has no place far enough away or dark enough for you to be hiding in. Hell will be easy compared to what any man will get that touches either of them!"

"Freckles, where are you?" demanded the Angel.

Soulsick with fear for her, Freckles went towards her and parted the bushes so that she might enter.

She came through apparently without giving him a glance, and the first words she said were:

"Why have the gang come so soon? I didn't know you expected them for three weeks yet. Or is this some special tree that Mr. McLean needs to fill an order right now?"

Freckles hesitated. Would a man dare lie to save himself? No. But to save the Angel—surely that was different.

He opened his lips, but the Angel was capable of saving herself. She walked among them exactly as if she had been reared in a lumber-camp, and never waited for an answer.

"Why, your specimen-case!" she cried. "Look! Haven't you noticed that it's tipped over? Set it straight, quickly!"

A couple of the men stepped out and carefully righted the case.

"There! That's better," she said. "Freckles, I'm surprised at your being so careless. It would be a shame to break those lovely butterflies for one old tree!

"Is that a valuable tree? Why didn't you tell us last night that you were going to take a tree out this morning?

"Oh, say, did you put your case there to protect that tree from that stealing old Black Jack and his gang? I bet you did! Well, if that wasn't bright! What kind of a tree is it?"

"It's a golden oak," said Freckles.

"Like those they make dining-tables and sideboards from?"

"Yes."

"My! How interesting!" she cried. "I do not know a thing about timber, but my father wants me to learn just everything I can. I am going to ask him to let me come here and watch you until I know enough to boss a gang myself."

She looked round.

"Do you like to cut trees, gentlemen?" she asked with angelic sweetness.

Some of the men appeared foolish and some grim, but one managed to say that he did.

Then the Angel's eyes turned full on Black Jack, and she gave the most beautiful little start of astonishment.

"Oh! I almost thought you were a ghost!" she cried. "But I see now that you are here really and truly. Were you ever in Colorado?"

"No," said Black Jack.

"I see you aren't the same man," said the Angel. "You know, we were in Colorado last year, and there was a cowboy that was the handsomest man anywhere round. He'd come riding into town every night, and all we girls just adored him! Oh, but he was a beauty!

"I thought at first glance you were really he, but I see now he wasn't nearly so tall nor so broad as you, and only half as handsome."

The men burst into a roar of laughter and Black Jack flushed crimson. The Angel joined in the laughter.

"Well, I'll leave it to you! Isn't he handsome?" she challenged. "As for that cowboy's face, it couldn't be compared with yours.

"The only trouble with you is that your clothes are spoiling you. It's the dress those cowboys wear that makes half their looks. If you were properly clothed, you could break the heart of the prettiest girl in the country."

With one accord the other men focussed on Black Jack, and for the first time realised that he was a superb specimen of manhood, for he stood six feet tall, was broad and well-rounded, and had dark, even skin, big black eyes, and full red lips.

"I'll tell you what!" exclaimed the Angel. "I'd just love to see you on horseback. Nothing sets a handsome man off so splendidly. Do you ride?"

"Yes," said Black Jack.

His eyes were burning on the Angel as if he would fathom the depths of her soul.

"Well," said the Angel winsomely, "I know just what I wish you'd do. I wish you would let your hair grow a little longer.

"Then wear a blue flannel shirt a little open

at the throat, a red tie, and a broad-brimmed felt hat, and ride past my house in the evenings.

"I'm always at home then, and almost always on the verandah, and, oh! but I would like to see you! Will you do that for me?"

It is impossible to describe the art with which the Angel put the question. She was looking straight into Black Jack's face, coarse and hardened with sin and careless living, which was now taking on a wholly different expression.

The evil lines of it were softening and fading under her clear gaze. A dull red flamed into his bronze cheeks, and his eyes were growing brightly tender.

"Yes," he said, and the glance he shot at the men was of such a nature that no one saw fit even to change countenance.

"Oh, goody!" she cried, tilting on her toes. "I'll ask all the girls to come and see, but they needn't stick in! We can get along without them, can't we?"

Jack leaned towards her. He was the charmed, fluttering bird, and the Angel was the snake.

"Well, I rather guess!" he cried.

The Angel drew a deep breath and surveyed him rapturously.

"My, but you're tall!" she said. "Do you suppose I ever will grow to reach your shoulders?"

She stood on tiptoe and measured the distance with her eyes. Then she fell into timid confusion, and her glance sought the ground.

"I wish I could do something, ... " she half-whispered.

Black Jack seemed to increase an inch in height.

"What?" he asked hoarsely.

"Lariat Bill always used to have a bunch of red flowers in his shirt-pocket, and the red lit up his dark eyes and olive cheeks and made him splendid. May I put a bunch of red flowers on you?"

The Angel knelt beside Freckle's flower-bed and recklessly tore up by the roots a big bunch of foxfire.

"These stems are so tough and sticky," she said. "I can't break them. Loan me your knife," she ordered Freckles.

As she reached for the knife, her back was for one second towards the men. She looked into his eyes and deliberately winked.

She severed the stems, tossed the knife to Freckles, and, walking to Black Jack, laid the flowers over his heart.

Freckles broke into a sweat of agony. He had said she would be safe in a herd of howling savages. Would she?

If Black Jack even made a motion towards touching her, Freckles knew that from somewhere he would muster the strength to kill him.

He mentally measured the distance to where his club lay and set his muscles for a spring. But no—by the splendour of God!

The big fellow was baring his head with a hand that was unsteady. The Angel pulled one of the long silver pins from her hat and fastened her flowers securely.

Freckles was quaking. What was to come next? What was she planning, and, oh! did she understand the danger of her presence among those men and the real necessity for action?

As the Angel stepped from Black Jack, she

turned her head to one side and peered at him, just as Freckles had seen the little yellow fellow do on the line a hundred times.

"Well, that does the trick!" she said. "Isn't that fine? See how it sets him off, boys? Don't you forget the tie is to be red, and the first ride must be soon. I can't wait very long.

"Now I must go. The Bird Woman will be ready to start, and she will come here hunting me next, for she is busy today. What did I come here for anyway?"

She glanced round enquiringly, and several of the men laughed! Oh, the delight of it. She had forgotten her errand for him!

Black Jack had a second increase in height. The Angel glanced helplessly, as if seeking a clue.

Then her eyes fell, as if by accident, on Freckles, and she cried:

"Oh, I know now! It was those magazines the Bird Woman promised you.

"I came to tell you that we put them under the box where we hide things, at the entrance to the swamp, as we came in. I knew I would need my hands crossing the swamp, so I hid them there. You'll find them at the same old place."

Then Freckles spoke.

"It's mighty risky for you to be crossing the swamp alone," he said. "I'm surprised that the Bird Woman would be letting you try it. I know it's a little farther, but it's begging you I am to be going back by the trail. That's bad enough, but it's safer than the swamp."

The Angel laughed merrily.

"Oh, stop your nonsense!" she cried. "I'm not afraid! Not in the least! The Bird Woman didn't want me to try following a path that I'd been over only once, but I was sure I could do it, and I'm rather proud of the performance. You know, I'm not afraid!"

"No," said Freckles gently, "I know you're not; but that has nothing to do with the fact that your friends are afraid for you. On the trail you can see your way a bit ahead, and you've all the world a better chance if you meet a snake."

Then Freckles had an inspiration. He turned to Black Jack imploringly.

"You tell her!" he pleaded. "Tell her to go by the trail. She will for you."

The implication of this statement was so gratifying to Black Jack that he seemed again to expand and take on an increase before their very eyes.

"You bet!" exclaimed Black Jack.

And to the Angel:

"You better take Freckles' word for it, Miss. He knows the old swamp better than any of us, except me, and if he says 'go by the trail,' you'd best do it."

The Angel hesitated. She wanted to recross the swamp and try to reach the horse. She knew Freckles would brave any danger to save her from crossing the swamp alone, but she really was not afraid, and the trail added over a mile to the walk.

She knew the path. She intended to run for dear life the instant she felt herself from their sight, and besides, tucked in the folds of her blouse was a fine little 32-calibre revolver that her father had presented her for her share in what he was pleased to call her millinery exploit.

One last glance at Freckles showed her the agony in his eyes, and immediately she imagined he had some other reason. She would follow the trail.

"All right," she said, giving Black Jack a thrilling glance. "If you say so, I'll return by the trail to please you. Good-bye, everybody."

She lifted the bushes and started for the entrance.

"You damned fool! Stop her!" growled Wessner. "Keep her till we're loaded, anyhow. You're playing hell! Can't you see that when this thing is found out, there she'll be to ruin all of us. If you let her go, every man of us has got to cut, and some of us will be caught sure."

Black Jack sprang forward. Freckles' heart was muffled in his throat. The Angel seemed to divine Black Jack's coming. She was humming a little song.

She deliberately stopped and began pulling the heads of the curious grasses that grew all round her.

When she straightened, she took a step backwards and called:

"Ho! Freckles, the Bird Woman wants that natural-history pamphlet returned. It belongs to a set she is going to have bound. That's one of the reasons we put it under the box. You be sure to get them as you go home tonight, for fear it rains or becomes damp with the heavy dews."

"All right," said Freckles, but it was in a voice that he had never used before.

Then the Angel turned and shot a parting glance at Black Jack, and she was overpoweringly human and bewitchingly lovely.

"You won't forget that ride and the red tie," she half-asserted, half-questioned.

Black Jack lost his head entirely. Freckles was

his captive, but he was the Angel's, soul and body.

His face wore the holiest look it ever had known as he softly re-echoed Freckles' "All right."

With her head held well up, the Angel walked slowly away, and Black Jack wheeled on the men.

"Drop your damned staring and saw wood," he shouted. "Don't you know anything at all about how to treat a lady?"

The men muttered and threatened among themselves, but they fell to working desperately. Someone suggested that a man be sent to follow the Angel and to watch her and the Bird Woman leave the swamp.

Freckles' heart died within him, but Black Jack was in a delirium and past all caution.

He sneered as he said:

"If anybody follows her, I do, and I'm needed here among such a pack of idiots. There's no danger in that baby face. She wouldn't give me away! You double and work like forty, and me and Wessner will take the axes and begin to cut in on the other side."

"What about the noise?" asked Wessner.

"No difference about the noise," answered Black Jack. "She took us to be from McLean's gang, slick as grease. Make the chips fly!"

So all of them attacked the big tree.

Freckles sat on one of his benches and waited. In their haste to fell the tree and load it, so that the teamsters could start, and leave them free to attack another, they had forgotten to rebind him.

The Angel was on the trail and safely started. The cold perspiration made Freckles' temples clammy and ran in little streams down his chest.

It would take her a little more time to go by the trail, but her safety was Freckles' sole thought in urging her to take that way.

He tried to figure how long it would require to walk to the carriage. He wondered if the Bird Woman had unhitched the horse. In his thoughts he followed the Angel every step of the way.

He figured out when she would cross the path of the clearing, pass the deep pool where his "find-out" frog lived, cross Sleepy Snake Creek, and reach the carriage.

He wondered what she would say to the Bird Woman and how long it would take them to pack and get started. He knew now that they would understand, and that the Angel would try to get the Boss there in time to save his wager.

She never could do it, for the saw was more than half through and Jack and Wessner were cutting into the opposite side of the tree. It appeared as if they could get at least that tree felled before McLean could come, and if they did he would lose his wager.

When it was down, would they rebind him and leave him for Wessner to wreak his insane vengeance on, or would they take him along to the next tree and dispose of him when they had stolen all the timber they could?

Black Jack had said that he should not be touched until he had left. Surely he would not run all that risk for one tree, when he had marked many others of far greater value.

Freckles felt that he had some hope to cling to now, but he found himself praying that the Angel would hurry.

Once Black Jack came to Freckles and asked if he had any water. Freckles rose and showed him where he kept his drinking-water.

Black Jack drank in great gulps, and as he passed back the bucket he said:

"When a man's got a chance of catching a fine girl like that, he ought not to be mixed up in any dirty business. I wish to God I was out of this!"

Freckles answered heartily:

"I wish I was too!"

Black Jack stared at him a minute and then broke into a roar of rough laughter.

"Blest if I blame you," he said. "But you had your chance! We offered you a fair thing and you gave Wessner his answer. I ain't envying you when he gives you his."

"You're six men to one," answered Freckles. "It will be easy enough for you to be killing the body of me, but, curse you all, you can't blacken my soul!"

"Well, I'd give anything you could name if I had your honesty," said Black Jack.

When the mighty tree fell, the Limberlost shivered and screamed with the echo.

Freckles groaned in despair, but the gang took heart. That was so much accomplished.

Now, if they could leave quickly, they knew where to dispose of it safely, with no questions asked. Before the day was over they could remove three others, all suitable for veneer and worth far more than this.

Then they would leave Freckles to Wessner, and scatter for safety, with more money than they had ever dreamed of in their possession.

Chapter
Six

On the line, the Angel gave one backward glance at Black Jack, to see that he had returned to his work. Then she gathered her skirts above her knees and leaped forward on the run.

In the first three yards she passed Freckles' bicycle. Instantly she realised that that was why he had insisted on her coming by the trail. She seized it and jumped on. The seat was too high, but she was an expert rider and could catch the pedals as they came up.

She stopped at the Duncans' cabin long enough to remedy this; while working, she told Mrs. Duncan what was happening and asked her to follow the East Trail until she found the Bird Woman. She added that she was going after McLean and that Mrs. Duncan should tell the Bird Woman to leave the swamp as quickly as possible.

Even with her fear for Freckles to spur her, Sarah Duncan blanched and began shivering at the idea of facing the Limberlost. The Angel looked her in the eyes.

"No matter how afraid you are, you have to go," she said. "If you don't, the Bird Woman will go to Freckles' room, hunting me, and they will have trouble with her.

"If she isn't told to leave at once, they may follow me, and, finding I'm gone, do some terrible thing to Freckles.

"I can't go—that's flat—for if they caught me, then there'd be no one to go for help. You don't suppose they are going to take out the trees they're after and then leave Freckles to run and tell?

"They are going to murder the boy; that's what they are going to do. You run, and run for life! For Freckles' life! You can ride back with the Bird Woman."

The Angel saw Mrs. Duncan started, and then began her race.

Those awful miles of trail! Would they never end? She did not dare use the bicycle too roughly, for if it broke she never could arrive on time afoot.

The day was fearfully warm. The sun poured with the fierce baking heat of August. The bushes claimed her hat, and she did not stop for it.

Where it was at all possible, the Angel mounted and pounded over the trail again. She was panting for breath and almost worn out when she reached the level pike.

She had no idea how long she had been— and she had covered only two miles.

She leaned over the bars, almost standing on the pedals, racing with all the strength in her body. The blood surged in her ears and her head swam, but she kept a straight course, and rode and rode.

It seemed to her that she was standing still while the trees and houses were racing past her.

Once a farmer's big dog rushed angrily into the road and she swerved until she almost fell, but she regained her balance, and, setting her muscles, pedalled as fast as she could.

At last she lifted her head. Surely it could not be over a mile more.

She was reeling in the saddle, but she gripped the bars with new energy, and raced desperately. The sun beat on her bare head and hands. Just when she was choking with dust and almost prostrate with heat and exhaustion—*crash!* she ran into a broken bottle.

Snap! went the tyre, and the bike swerved and pitched over. The tired Angel rolled into the thick yellow dust of the road and lay quietly.

From afar, Duncan began to notice a strange dust-covered object in the road, as he headed towards town with the first load of the day's felling.

As he neared the Angel, he saw that it was a woman and a broken bicycle. He was beside her in an instant

He carried her to a shaded fence-corner, stretched her on the grass, and wiped the dust from the lovely face, which was all dirt-streaked, crimson, and bearing a startling whiteness round the mouth and nose.

He glanced at the Angel's tumbled clothing, and the silkiness of her hair, with its pale satin ribbon, and noticed that she had lost her hat. His lips tightened in an ominous quiver.

He left her and picked up the bicycle: it was as he had surmised. This, then, was Freckles' Swamp Angel. There was trouble in the Limberlost, and she had broken down racing to Mc-Lean.

Duncan turned the bays into a fence-corner, tied one of them, unharnessed the other, fastened up the trace-chains, and hurried to the nearest farm-house to send help to the Angel.

He found a woman, who took a bottle of camphor, a jug of water, and some towels, and started on the run.

Then Duncan put the bay to speed and raced for camp.

The Angel, left alone, lay still for a second, then shivered and opened her eyes. She saw that she was on the grass, with a broken bicycle beside her. Instantly she realised that someone had carried her there and gone for help.

She sat up and looked round. Her eyes fell on the load of logs and the one horse. Someone was riding for help for her!

"Oh, poor Freckles!" she wailed. "They may be killing him by now. Oh, how much time have I wasted?"

She hurried to the other bay, and her fingers flew as she set him free. Snatching up a big black snake-whip that lay on the ground, she caught the harness and stretched along the horse's neck, and the fine, big fellow felt on his back the quality of the lash that Duncan was accustomed to crack over him.

He was frightened, and galloped at top speed.

On the road, the Angel passed a wildly waving, screaming woman, and a little later a man riding as if he too were in great haste.

The man called to her, but she only lay lower and slashed away with the whip.

Soon the hoofs of the man's horse sounded farther and farther away.

At the South Camp they were loading a second waggon, when the Angel appeared riding one of Duncan's bays, lathered and dripping.

She cried:

"Everybody go to Freckles! There are thieves stealing trees and they have him bound. They're going to kill him!"

She wheeled the horse and headed for the Limberlost. The alarm sounded over the camp. The gang were not unprepared. McLean sprang to Nellie's back and raced after the Angel.

As they passed Duncan, he wheeled and followed. Soon the pike was an irregular procession of bare-back riders, wildly driving flying horses towards the swamp.

The Boss rode neck-and-neck with the Angel. Repeatedly he commanded her to stop and fall out of line, until he remembered that he would need her to lead him to Freckles.

Then he gave up and rode beside her, for she was sending the bay at as sharp a pace as the other horses could keep. He could see that she was not hearing him.

He glanced back and saw that Duncan was close. There was something terrifying in the appearance of the big man and the way he sat his beast and rode. It would be a sad day for the man on whom Duncan's wrath broke.

There were four others close behind him, so McLean took heart and raced beside the Angel.

Over and over he asked her where the trouble was, but he could get no reply. She only gripped the reins, leaned along the bay's neck, and slashed away with the black snake-whip.

The steaming horse, with crimson nostrils and heaving sides, stretched out and ran for home with all the speed there was in him.

When they passed the cabin, the Bird Woman's carriage was there and Mrs. Duncan was in the door, wringing her hands. But the Bird Woman was nowhere to be seen.

The Angel sent the bay along the path that turned in to the trail to the west. The men bunched and followed her.

When she reached the entrance to Freckles' room, there were four men with her and two more very close behind.

She slid from the horse and, snatching the little revolver from her pocket, darted for the bushes.

McLean caught the men back, and with drawn weapon he pressed beside her.

There they stopped, in astonishment.

The Bird Woman blocked the entrance. Over a small limb lay her revolver, and it was trained at short range on Black Jack and Wessner, who stood with their hands above their heads.

Freckles, with blood streaming down his face, from an ugly cut in his temple, was gagged and bound to the tree again, and the remainder of the men were gone.

Black Jack was raving as a maniac, and when they looked closer it was only the left arm that he raised.

His right, with the hand shattered, hung helpless at his side, and his revolver lay at Freckles' feet. Wessner's weapon was in his belt and beside him was Freckles' club.

Freckles' face was white, with colourless lips,

but in his eyes was the strength of undying courage.

McLean pushed past the Bird Woman, crying:

"Hold steady on them for just one minute more!"

He snatched the revolver from Wessner's belt and stooped for Black Jack's.

At that instant the Angel rushed past. She tore the gag from Freckles, and, seizing the rope knotted on his chest, she tugged at it desperately. Under her fingers it gave way, and she hurled it to McLean.

The men were crowding in, and Duncan seized Wessner. As the Angel saw Freckles stand out, free, she reached out her arms to him and pitched forward.

A fearful oath burst from the lips of Black Jack. To save his life Freckles could not have avoided the glance of triumph he gave Black Jack, as he folded the Angel in his arms and stretched her on the mosses.

The Bird Woman cried out sharply for water as she ran to them. Someone sprang for that, and another to break open the case for brandy.

As McLean rose from binding Wessner, there was a cry that Black Jack was escaping.

He was already far into the swamp, running in leaping bounds for its densest part. Every man who could be spared plunged after him.

Other members of the gang were sent to follow the tracks of the waggons. The teamsters had driven from the west entrance, and, crossing the swale, had taken the same route that the Bird Woman and the Angel had taken before them.

There had been ample time for the drivers to reach the road; after that, they could take any one of four directions.

Traffic was heavy, and lumber-waggons were passing almost constantly, so the men turned back and joined the more exciting hunt for a man. The remainder of the gang joined them, as well as farmers from the pike and travellers attracted by the disturbance.

Watchers were set all along the trail at short intervals, and with lighted torches they patrolled the line and roads through the swamp that night.

The next day McLean headed as thorough a search as he felt could be made of one side, while Duncan covered the other; but Black Jack could not be found.

Spies were set round his home, in Wildcat Hollow, to ascertain if he reached there or aid was being sent from any direction to him; but it was soon clear that his relatives were ignorant of his hiding-place and were searching for him.

Great is the elasticity of youth. A hot bath and a sound night's sleep renewed Freckles' strength, and it needed but little more to work the same result with the Angel.

Freckles was on the trail early the next morning. Besides a crowd of people anxious to witness Black Jack's capture, he found four stalwart guards, one at each turn.

In his heart he was compelled to admit that he was glad to have them there.

Close to noon, McLean placed his men in the charge of Duncan, and, taking Freckles, drove to town to see how it fared with the Angel.

McLean visited a greenhouse and bought an

armload of its finest products, but Freckles would have none of them. He would carry his message in a glowing mass of the Limberlost's first goldenrod.

The Bird Woman received them, and in answer to their eager enquiries she said that the Angel was in no way seriously injured, only so bruised and shaken that their Doctor had ordered her to lie quietly for the day.

Though she was sore and stiff, they were having work to keep her in bed. Her callers sent up their flowers with their grateful regards, and the Angel promptly returned word that she wanted to see them.

She turned to Freckles. "And you must be the happiest man alive, because you have kept your trust. Go look where I tell you and you'll find the logs. I can see just about where they are.

"When they go up that steep little hill into the next woods after the corn-field, why, they could unloose the chains and the logs would roll from the waggons themselves.

"Now, you go look; and, Mr. McLean, you do feel that Freckles has been brave and faithful? You won't love him any less even if you don't find the logs—"

The Angel's nerve gave way and she began to cry.

Freckles could not endure it.

He almost ran from the room, with tears in his eyes; but McLean took the Angel from the Bird Woman's arms, and kissed her brave little face, and stroked her hair, and petted her into quietness before he left.

As they drove to the swamp, McLean so earnestly seconded all that the Angel had said that he soon had the boy feeling much better.

"Freckles, your Angel has a spice of the devil in her, but she's superb! You needn't spend any time questioning or bewailing anything she does. Just worship blindly, my boy. By Heaven! She has sense, courage, and beauty for half-a-dozen girls."

"It's altogether right you are, Sir," affirmed Freckles heartily. "There's no question but that the series is over now."

"Don't think it!" answered McLean. "The Bird Woman is working for success, and success along any line is not won by being scared out.

"She will be back on the usual day, and ten to one the Angel will be with her. They are made of pretty stern stuff, and they don't scare worth a cent.

"Just before I left, I told the Bird Woman it would be safe; and it will. You may do your usual walking, but those four guards are there to remain. They are under your orders absolutely.

"They are prohibited from firing on any bird or molesting anything that you want to protect, but there they stay, and this time it is useless for you to say one word.

"I have listened to your pride too long. You are too precious to me, and that voice of yours is too precious to the world to run any more risks."

"I am sorry to have anything spoil the series," said Freckles, "and I'd love them to be coming, the Angel especial, but it can't be. You'll have to tell them so.

"You see, Black Jack would have been ready

to stake his life that my Angel meant what she said and did to him.

"When the teams pulled out, Wessner seized me, and he and Black Jack went to quarelling over whether they should finish me then or take me to the next tree they were for felling. Between them they were pulling me round and hurting me bad.

"Wessner wanted to get at me right then, and Jack said he shouldn't be touching me till the last tree was out and all the rest of them gone.

"I'm believing Black Jack really hated to see me done for in the beginning; and I think, too, he was afraid if Wessner finished me then he'd lose his nerve and cut, and they couldn't be managing the felling without him; anyway, they were hauling me round like I was already past all feeling, and they tied me up again.

"To keep my courage up, I twits Wessner about having to tie me and needing another man to help handle me. I told him what I'd do to him if I was free, and he grabs up my own club and lays open my head with it.

"When the blood came streaming, it set Black Jack raving, and he cursed and damned Wessner for a coward and a softy. Then Wessner turned on Black Jack and gives it to him for letting the Angel make a fool of him.

"Tells him she was just playing with him, and beyond all manner of doubt she'd gone after you, and there was nothing to do on account of his foolishness but finish me, get out, and let the rest of the timber go, for likely you was on the way right then.

"It drove Black Jack plum crazy. I don't think he was for having a doubt of the Angel before, but then he just raved. He grabbed out his gun and turned on Wessner.

"*Spang!* It went out of his fist, and the order comes, 'Hands up!' Wessner reached for kingdom come like he was expecting to grab hold and pull himself up. Jack puts up what he has left.

"Then, just like a snake hissing, he spits out what he'll do to her for playing with him.

"He did get away, and, with his strength, that wound in his hand won't be bothering him long. He'll do to me just what he said, and when he hears it really was she that went for you, why, he'll keep his oath about her.

"He's lived in the swamp all his life, Sir, and everybody says it's always been the home of cutthroats, outlaws, and runaways. He knows its most secret places as none of the others.

"He's alive. He's in there now, Sir. Some way he'll keep alive.

"If you'd seen his face, all scarlet with passion, twisted with pain, and black with hate, and heard him swearing that oath, you'd know it was a sure thing.

"I ain't done with him yet, and I've brought this awful thing on her."

"And I haven't begun with him yet," said McLean, setting his teeth. "I've been way too slow and too easy, believing there'd be no greater harm than the loss of a tree.

"I've sent for a couple of first-class detectives. We will put them on his track, and rout him out and rid the country of him.

"I don't propose for him to stop either our work or our pleasure. As for his being in the swamp now, I don't believe it. He'd find a way out last night, in spite of us.

"Don't you worry! I am at the helm now, and I'll see to that gentleman in my own way."

"I wish to my soul you had seen and heard him!" said Freckles, unconvinced.

They entered the swamp, taking the route followed by the Bird Woman and the Angel. They really did find the logs, almost where the Angel had predicted they would be.

Then McLean sent for a pack of bloodhounds and put them on the trail of Black Jack. They clung to it, on and on, into the depths of the swamp, leading their followers through what had been considered impassable and impenetrable ways, and finally round near the west entrance and into the swale.

Here the dogs bellowed, raved, and fell over one another in their excitement. They raced back and forth from swamp to swale, but follow the scent farther they would not, even though cruelly driven.

At last their owner attributed their actions to snakes, and, as they were very valuable dogs, he abandoned the effort to urge them on.

So, all they really established was the fact that Black Jack had eluded their vigilance and crossed the trail sometime in the night. He had escaped to the swale; from there he probably had crossed the trail, and, reaching the lower end of the swamp, had found friends.

At any rate, it was a great relief to feel that he was not in the swamp, and it raised the spirits of every man on the line, though many of them expressed regrets that he, who was undoubtedly most to blame, should escape, and Wessner, who in the beginning was only his tool, should be left to punishment.

But for Freckles, with Black Jack's fearful oath ringing in his ears, there was neither rest nor peace.

He was almost ill when the day for the next study of the series arrived and he saw the Bird Woman and the Angel coming down the trail.

The guards of the East Line he left at their customary places, but those of the West Line he brought over and placed, one near Little Chicken's tree and the other at the carriage.

He was so firm about the Angel remaining in the carriage that he did not offer to have the horse unhitched. He went with the Bird Woman for the picture, which was the easiest matter it yet had been.

The placing of the guards and the unusual movement about the swamp had made Mr. and Mrs. Chicken timid, and they had not carried Little Chicken the customary amount of food.

Freckles, in the anxiety of the last few days, had neglected him, and he was so hungry that when the Bird Woman held up a sweet-bread, although he had started for the recesses of the log at her coming, he changed his mind.

With opened beak, he waited anxiously for the treat, and gave a study of great value, showing every point of his head and his wing and tail development as well.

When the Bird Woman proposed to look for other subjects close to the line, Freckles went so far as to tell her that Black Jack had made fearful threats against the Angel. He implored her to take the Angel home and keep her under unceasing guard until Black Jack was located.

He wanted to tell her all about it, but he knew how dear the Angel was to her, and he dreaded to burden her with his fears when they might prove groundless.

Without saying anything, he allowed her to go, and then blamed himself fiercely that he had done so.

*　　*　　*

McLean rode to the Limberlost, and, stopping in the shade, sat waiting for Freckles, whose hour for passing the foot of the lease had come.

Along the North Line came Freckles, fairly staggering. When he turned east and reached Sleepy Snake Creek, sliding through the swale as the long black snake for which it was named, he sat on the bridge and closed his burning eyes, but they would not remain shut.

As if pulled by wires, his heavy lids flew open, and the outraged nerves and muscles of his body danced, twitched, and tingled.

He bent forward and idly watched the limpid little stream flowing beneath his feet.

Freckles sat so quietly that soon the brim of his hat was covered with snake-feeders, rasping their crisp wings and singing as they rested. Some of them settled on the club, and one on his shoulder.

Then he hurried on the East Trail as fast as his tottering legs would carry him to the Boss. He took off his hat, wiped his forehead, and stood silently under the eyes of McLean.

The Boss was dumbfounded. Mrs. Duncan had led him to expect that he would find a change in Freckles, but this was almost deathly.

The fact was apparent that the boy scarcely knew what he was doing.

Without a thought of preliminaries, McLean leaned over in the saddle and drew Freckles to him.

"My poor lad!" he said. "My poor, dear lad! Tell me and we will try to right it!"

"It's the Angel, Sir," he said.

Instinctively McLean's grip on him tightened, and Freckles looked into the Boss's face in wonder.

"I tried hard the other day," said Freckles, "and I couldn't seem to make you see. It's only that there hasn't been an hour, waking or sleeping, since the day she parted the bushes and looked into my room, that the face of her hasn't been before me, with all the tenderness, beauty, and mischief of it.

"This last time, she walked into that gang of murderers, took their leader, and twisted him to the will of her. She outdone him and raced the life almost out of her trying to save me.

"If any evil comes to her through Black Jack, it comes from her angel-like goodness to me. Somewhere he's hiding! Somewhere he is waiting for his chance!

"Somewhere he is reaching out for her! I tell you I cannot, I dare not, be bearing it longer!"

"Freckles, be quiet!" said McLean, his eyes humid and his voice quivering with the pity of it all.

"Believe me, I will see that she is fully protected every hour of the day and night until Black Jack is located and disposed of."

Together they turned in to the trail.

McLean noticed and spoke of the big black "chickens."

"They've been hanging round out there for several days past," said Freckles. "I'll tell you what I think it means. I think the old rattler has killed something too big for him to swallow, and he's keeping guard and won't let my 'chickens' have it."

Suddenly McLean turned on him with blanching face.

"Freckles!" he cried.

"You think it's Black Jack!" shuddered Freckles.

He caught up his club and plunged into the swale. Reaching for his revolver, McLean followed.

The "chickens" circled higher at their coming, and the big snake lifted its head and rattled angrily. It sank in sinuous coils at the report of McLean's revolver; then together he and Freckles stood beside Black Jack. His fate was evident and most horrible.

"Come," said the Boss at last. "We don't dare touch him. We will get a sheet from Mrs. Duncan and tuck it over him, to keep these swarms of insects away, and set a man on guard while we find the officers."

As he and Freckles drove towards town, McLean said:

"My soul is sick with the horror of this thing."

"Did you ever hear of anyone, excepting him, that ever tried to locate any trees?" asked Freckles.

"No, I never did," said McLean. "I am sure

there was no one besides him. Black Jack knew the swamp better than anyone else here. I think his sole intention in forcing me to discharge him from my gang was to come here and try to steal timber. We had no idea, when we took the lease, what a gold-mine it was."

"That's exactly what Wessner said that first day," said Freckles eagerly. "That 'twas a 'gold mine'! He said he knew a man who had told him so, and if I would hold off and let them get the marked ones, there were a dozen they could take out in few days."

"Freckles!" cried McLean. "You don't mean a dozen!"

"That's what he said, Sir—a dozen. This makes three they've tried, so there must be nine more marked, and several of them just for being fine."

"Well, I wish I knew which they are," said McLean, "so I could get them out first."

"I have been thinking," said Freckles. "I believe I could be finding some of them."

"Good!" said McLean. "We will do that. You may begin as soon as you are rested.

"Have you stopped to think of all we owe her, my boy?"

"Yes; we owe the Angel a lot," said Freckles. "I owe her my life and my honour."

Chapter
Seven

Freckles and the Angel started towards the cabin. Every few minutes they stopped to investigate something or to chatter over some natural-history wonder.

The Angel had quick eyes, and she seemed to see everything; but Freckles' were even quicker, for life itself had depended on their sharpness ever since the beginning of his work at the swamp. They saw it at the same time.

"Looks as if someone has been making a flag-pole," said the Angel. "Freckles, what would anyone cut a tree as small as that for?"

"I don't know," said Freckles.

"Well, but I want to know!" said the Angel. "No one came all the way out here and cut it just for fun. They've taken it away. Let's go back and see if we can see it anywhere there."

She turned, retraced her footsteps, and began eagerly searching. Freckles did the same.

"There it is!" he exclaimed at last. "Leaning just as naturally against the trunk of the big maple."

"Yes, and leaning there has killed a patch of bark," said the Angel. "See how dried it appears?"

Freckles stared at her.

"Angel!" he shouted. "I bet you it's a marked tree!"

"Course it is!" cried the Angel. "No one would cut that sapling and carry it away there and lean it up for nothing.

"I'll tell you! This is one of Black Jack's marked trees. He climbed up there above anyone's head, peeled the bark, and cut into the grain enough to be sure.

"Can you climb to that place?"

"Yes," said Freckles; "if I take off my wading-boots, I can."

"Then take them off," said the Angel. "And do hurry! Can't you see that I am almost crazy to know if this tree is a marked one?"

They pushed the sapling over and a piece of bark as big as the crown of Freckles' hat fell away.

Freckles reached the opening and then slid rapidly to the ground. He was almost breathless and his eyes were flashing.

"The bark's been cut clean with a knife, the sap scraped away, and a big chip taken out deep. The trunk is the twistiest thing you ever saw. It's as full of eyes as a bird is of feathers!"

The Angel was dancing and shaking his hand.

"Oh, Freckles!" she cried. "I'm so delighted that you found it!"

The clear, ringing echo of strongly swung axes came crashing through the Limberlost.

" 'Tis the gang!" shouted Freckles. "They're clearing a place to make camp. Let's go help!"

"Hadn't we better mark that tree again?" cautioned the Angel. "It's way in here. There's such a lot of them, and all so much alike. We'd feel good and green if we found it and then lost it."

Freckles lifted the sapling to replace it, but the Angel motioned him away.

"Get out your hatchet," she said. "I predict this is the most valuable tree in the swamp. You found it. I'm going to play that you're my knight. Now, you nail my colours on it."

She reached up, and pulling a blue bow from her hair, she untied it and doubled it against the tree.

Freckles turned his eyes from her and managed the fastening with shaking fingers.

The Angel had called him her knight! Dear Lord, how he loved her!

When they had gone a little distance they both looked back, and the morning breeze set the bit of blue to waving them a farewell. Angel gave him her hand, and as two children they broke into a run as they caught up with the gang.

"Good-morning, Mr. Boss of the Limberlost!" she greeted McLean.

The gang shouted, and McLean bowed profoundly before her.

"Everyone listen!" cried the Angel, climbing up onto a roll of canvass. "I have something to say! Freckles has been guarding here over a year now, and he presents the Limberlost to you, with every tree in it saved; and he has this morning just located the rarest one of them all: it is the

one from the East Line, which Wessner spoke of
the first day. Now, all together! Everyone! Hurrah
for Freckles!"

Then they cheered together.

"Tell me, Angel," the Boss said jestingly. "I
think I have a right to know. Who really did locate that tree?"

"Freckles," she answered promptly and emphatically.

"But he says just as positively that it was you.
I don't understand."

"I'll tell you, just word for word, how it happened," she said, "and then you shall decide, and
Freckles and I will agree with you."

When   she   had   finished   her   version,
she laughingly said:

"Tell us, 'oh, most learned judge'! which of us
located that tree."

"Blest if I know who located it!" exclaimed
McLean. "But I have a pretty accurate idea as to
who put the blue ribbon on it."

*   *   *

It was several days before they completed a
road to the noble, big tree and were ready to fell
it.

When the sawing began, Freckles was watching down the road where it met the trail leading
from Little Chicken's tree. He had gone to the
tree ahead of the gang and taken down the blue
ribbon. Carefully folded, it now lay over his heart.

The saw was out and the men were sending
ringing blows into the felling side of the tree
when the Boss rode in.

His first word was to enquire for the Angel.
When Freckles said she had not yet come, the

Boss at once gave orders to stop work on the tree until she arrived; for he felt that she virtually had located it, and if she desired to see it felled, she should.

As the men stepped back, a stiff morning breeze caught the tree-top, which towered high above.

There was an ominous grinding at the base, a shiver of the mighty trunk, and directly in line of its fall the bushes swung apart and the laughing face of the Angel looked on them.

A groan of horror burst from the dry throats of the men, and, reading the agony in their faces, she stopped short, glanced up, and understood.

"South!" shouted McLean. "Run south!"

The Angel was helpless. It was apparent that she did not know which way was south.

There was another slow shiver of the big tree. The remainder of the gang stood motionless, but Freckles sprang past the trunk and went leaping in big bounds.

He caught up the Angel and dashed through the thicket for safety. The swaying trunk was half-over when, just for an instant, a nearby tree stayed its fall.

They saw Freckles' foot catch, and then with the Angel he plunged headlong.

A terrible cry broke from the men and McLean covered his face.

Instantly Freckles was up, with the Angel in his arms, struggling on. The outer limbs were on them when they saw Freckles hurl the Angel face down into the muck, as far from him as he could send her.

Springing after, in an attempt to cover her body with his own, he whirled to see if they were still in danger, and with outstretched arms he braced himself for the shock.

The branches shut them from sight, and the awful crash rocked the earth.

McLean and Duncan ran with axes and saws. The remainder of the gang followed, and they worked desperately. It seemed an age before they caught a glimpse of the Angel's blue dress, and it renewed their vigour.

Duncan fell on his knees beside her and with his hands tore the muck from underneath her. In a few seconds he dragged her out, choking and stunned, but surely not fatally hurt.

Freckles lay a little farther under the tree, a big limb pinning him down. His eyes were wide open and he was perfectly conscious.

Duncan began mining beneath him, but Freckles stopped him.

"You can't be moving me," he said. "You must cut off the limb and lift it. I know."

Two men ran for the big saw. A number of them laid hold of the limb and bore up. In a little time it was removed, and Freckles lay free.

The men bent over to lift him, but he motioned them away.

"Don't be touching me until I rest a bit," he pleaded.

Then he twisted his head until he saw the Angel, who was wiping the muck from her eyes and face on the skirt of her dress.

"Try to get up," he begged.

McLean laid hold of the Angel and helped her to her feet.

"Do you think any bones are broken?" Freckles asked with a gasp.

The Angel shook her head and wiped away more muck.

"You see if you can find any, Sir," Freckles commanded.

The Angel yielded herself to McLean's touch, and he assured Freckles that she was not seriously injured.

Freckles settled back, a smile of ineffable tenderness on his face.

"Thank the Lord!" he whispered hoarsely.

The Angel broke away from McLean.

"Now, Freckles, you!" she cried. "It's your turn. Please get up!"

A pitiful spasm swept Freckles' face. The sight of it washed every vestige of colour from the Angel's. She took hold of his hands.

"Freckles, get up!"

It was half-command, half-entreaty.

"Easy, Angel, easy! Let me rest a bit first!" implored Freckles.

She knelt beside him, and he reached his arm round her and drew her close.

He looked at McLean in an agony of entreaty that brought the Boss to his knees on the other side.

"Oh, Freckles!" McLean cried. "Not that! Surely we can do something! We must! Let me see!"

He tried to unfasten Freckles' neck-band, but his fingers shook so clumsily that the Angel pushed them away and herself laid Freckles' chest bare.

With one hasty glance, she gathered the clothing together and slipped her arm under his head. Freckles lifted eyes of agony to hers.

"You see?" he said.

The Angel nodded dumbly.

Freckles turned to McLean.

"Thank you for everything," he said, panting. "Where are the boys?"

"They are all here," said the Boss, "except Mrs. Duncan and the Bird Woman, who have gone for a doctor."

"It's no use trying to do anything," said Freckles.

He turned with a smile of adoring tenderness to the Angel. She was ghastly white and her eyes were dull and glazed.

Instantly she laid her lips on his forehead, then on each cheek, and then in a long kiss on his lips.

Then McLean bent over him.

"Freckles," he said brokenly, "you will never know how I love you. You won't go without saying good-bye to me?"

That word stung the Angel to quick comprehension. She started as if rousing from sleep.

"Good-bye?" she cried sharply.

Her eyes widened and the colour rushed into her white face.

"Good-bye! Why, what do you mean? Who's saying good-bye? Where could Freckles go when he is hurt like this, save to the Hospital?"

"It's no use, Angel," said Freckles. "I'm thinking every bone in my breast is smashed. You'll have to be letting me go!"

"I will not," said the Angel flatly. "It's no use wasting precious time talking about it. You are alive, you are breathing, and no matter how badly your bones are broken, what are great Surgeons for but to fix you up and make you well again?"

"Oh, Angel!" Freckles moaned. "I can't. You don't know how bad it is. I'll die the minute you try to lift me!"

"Of course you will, if you make up your mind to do it," said the Angel. "But if you are determined you won't, and set yourself to breathing deep and strong, and hang on to me tight, I can get you out.

"You have to do it, Freckles, no matter how it hurts you, for you did this for me, and now I must save you. So you might as well promise."

She bent over him, trying to smile encouragement with her fear-stiffened lips.

"You will promise, Freckles?"

Big drops of cold sweat ran together on Freckles' temples.

"You are going to promise me," she said. "'Angel I give you my word of honour that I will keep right on breathing.' Do you say it?"

Freckles hesitated.

"Freckles!" the Angel commanded imploringly. "You must say it!"

"Yes," said Freckles, gasping.

The Angel sprang to her feet.

"Then that's all right," she said to the men, with a tinge of her old-time briskness. "You just keep sawing away like a steam-engine, and I will do all the remainder."

She dropped into the muck beside Freckles and began stroking his hair and hand. He lay with his face of agony turned to hers, and fought to smother the groans that would tell her what he was suffering.

When they stood ready to lift him, the Angel bent over him in a passion of tenderness.

"Dear old Limberlost Guard, we're going to

lift you now," she said. "I suspect you will faint from the pain of it, but we will be just as easy as ever we can, and don't you dare forget your promise!"

A whimsical half-smile touched Freckles' quivering lips.

"I am ready," he said.

With the first touch his eyes closed, a mighty groan wrenched from him, and he lay senseless.

The Angel gave Duncan one panic-stricken look, then she set her lips and gathered her forces again.

"I guess that's a good thing," she said. "Maybe he won't feel how we are hurting him. Oh, boys, are you being quick and gentle?"

She stepped to the side of the cot and bathed Freckles' face. Taking his hand in hers, she gave the word to start.

The Bird Woman insisted upon taking the Angel into the carriage and following the stretcher, but she refused to leave Freckles, and she suggested that the Bird Woman drive ahead, pack them some clothing, and be at the station ready to accompany them to Chicago.

All the way the Angel walked beside the stretcher, shading Freckles' face with a branch and holding his hand. At every pause to change carriers she moistened his face and lips, and counted each breath with heartbreaking anxiety.

When the train pulled in and the gang placed Freckles aboard, big Duncan made a place for the Angel beside the stretcher.

With the best Physician to be found, and with the Bird Woman and McLean in attendance, the four-hour run to Chicago began.

At five o'clock Freckles lay stretched on the

operating-table of Lake View Hospital, while three of the greatest Surgeons in Chicago bent over him.

The Angel had been told that the word the Surgeon brought that morning would be final, so she curled in a window-seat, dropped the curtains behind her, and, in dire anxiety, awaited the opening of that closed door.

Just as it opened, McLean came hurrying down the hall, and with one glance at the Surgeon's face he stepped back in dismay.

"Is he dying?" demanded McLean.

"He is," said the Surgeon. "He will not live this day out, unless some strong reaction sets in at once. He is so low that, preferring death to life, nature cannot overcome his inertia. If he is to live, he must be made to desire life. Now he undoubtedly wishes for death to come quickly."

"Then he must die," said McLean.

His broad shoulders shook convulsively, and his strong hands opened and closed mechanically.

"Does that mean that you know what he desires, and cannot, or will not, supply it?" the Surgeon asked.

McLean groaned in misery.

"It means," he said desperately, "that I know what he wants, but it is as far removed from my power to help him as it would be to give him a star. The thing for which he will die he can never have."

"Then you must prepare for the end very shortly," said the Surgeon, turning away abruptly.

McLean caught his arm roughly.

"It is that child that he wants! He worships

her to adoration, and, knowing he can never be anything to her, he prefers death to life. In God's name, what can I do about it?"

"Barring that missing hand, I never examined a finer man," said the Surgeon, "and she seems perfectly devoted to him; why can he not have her?"

"Why?" echoed McLean. "Why? Well, for many reasons! I told you he was my son. You probably knew that he was not. A little over a year ago I never had seen him. He joined one of my lumber-gangs from the road.

"He is a stray, left at one of your Homes for the Friendless here in Chicago. When he grew up, the Superintendent bound him to a brutal man.

"He ran away and landed in one of my lumber-camps. He has no name or knowledge of legal birth.

"The Angel—we have talked of her. You see what she is, physically and mentally. She is an idolised, petted, only child, and there is great wealth.

"Life holds everything for her, nothing for him. He sees it more plainly than anyone else could. There is nothing for the boy but death, if it is the Angel that is required to save him."

The Angel stood between them.

"Well, I just guess not!" she cried. "If Freckles wants me, all he has to do is to say so, and he can have me!"

The amazed men stepped back, staring at her.

"That he will never say," said McLean at last. "And you don't understand, Angel.

"I don't know how you came here, and I

wouldn't have had you hear that for the world; but since you have, dear girl, you must be told that it isn't your friendship or your kindness Freckles wants—it is your love."

The Angel looked straight into the great Surgeon's eyes with her clear, steady orbs of blue, and then into McLean's with unwavering frankness.

"Well, I do love him," she said simply.

McLean's arms dropped helplessly.

"You don't understand," he reiterated patiently. "It isn't the love of a friend, or a comrade, or a sister, that Freckles wants from you; it is the love of a sweetheart."

Then the Angel grew splendid. A rosy flush swept the pallor of fear from her face, and her big eyes widened and dilated with intense lights.

She seemed to leap to the height and the dignity of superb womanhood before their wondering gaze.

"I do love Freckles, just as I say I do. I don't know anything about the love of sweethearts, but I love him with all the love in my heart, and I think that will satisfy him."

"Surely it should!" muttered the Surgeon.

"Can't I see how brave, trustworthy, and splendid he is?" the Angel asked. "Can't I see how his soul vibrates with his music, his love of beautiful things, and the pangs of loneliness and heart-hunger? My father is never unreasonable; he won't expect me not to love Freckles, or not to tell him so, if the telling will save him."

She darted past McLean into Freckles' rooms, closed the door, and turned the key.

Chapter Eight

Freckles lay on a flat pillow, his body immovable in a plaster cast, his maimed arm, as always, hidden.

His greedy gaze fastened at once on the Angel's face. She crossed to him with a light step and bent over him with infinite tenderness.

Her heart ached at the change in his appearance. He seemed so weak, heart-hungry, and so utterly hopeless and alone. She could see that the night had been one long terror.

The Angel dropped on her knees beside the bed, slipped her arm under the pillow, and, leaning over Freckles, set her lips on his forehead.

He smiled faintly, but his wistful face looked worse for it. It cut the Angel to the heart.

"Dear Freckles," she said, "there is a story in your eyes this morning. Will you tell me?"

Freckles drew a long, wavering breath.

"Angel," he begged, "be generous! Be thinking of me a little. I'm so homesick and worn out, dear Angel—be giving me back my promise. Let me go?"

"Why, Freckles!" The Angel faltered. "You don't know what you are asking. Let you go! I cannot! I love you better than anyone, Freckles. I think you are the very finest person I ever knew. I have our lives all planned."

Her voice dropped as she went on:

"I want you to be educated and learn all there is to know about singing, just as soon as you are well enough. By the time you have completed your education I will have finished college, and then I want . . ."

She choked on the words.

"I want you to be my real knight, Freckles, and come to me and tell me that you . . . like me—a little. I have been counting on you for my sweetheart from the very first, Freckles. I can't give you up, unless you don't like me. But you do like me . . . just a little . . . don't you, Freckles?"

Freckles lay, whiter than the coverlet, his staring eyes on the ceiling and his breath wheezing between dry lips.

The Angel awaited his answer a second, and when none came she dropped her crimsoning face beside him on the pillow and whispered in his ear:

"Freckles, I . . . I'm trying to make love to you. Oh, can't you help me just a little bit? It's awful hard all alone! I love you. I must have you, and now I guess—I guess maybe I'd better kiss you next."

She lifted her shamed face and bravely laid her feverish, quivering lips on his. Her breath, like clover-bloom, was in his nostrils, and her hair touched his face.

"Freckles," she said, panting, "Freckles! I didn't think it was in you to be mean!"

"Mean, Angel! Mean to you?" Freckles gasped.

"Yes," said the Angel. "Downright mean. When one kisses you, if you had any mercy at all you'd kiss back, just a little bit. You aren't too sick to help me just a little, Freckles?"

His chin pointed ceilingwards and his head rocked on the pillow.

"Oh, Jesus!" burst from him in agony. "You ain't the only one that was crucified!"

The Angel caught Freckles' hand and carried it to her breast.

"Freckles!" she wailed in terror. "Freckles!"

Freckles' head rolled on in wordless suffering.

"Wait a bit, Angel?" he said at last, panting. "Be giving me a little time!"

"Tell me, Freckles," she whispered softly.

"If I can," said Freckles in biting agony. "It's just this: Angels are from above. Outcasts are from below. You have everything that loving, careful raising and money can give you. I have so much less than nothing that I don't suppose I had any right to be born. It's a sure thing—nobody wanted me afterwards, so of course they didn't before."

"If that's all you have to say, Freckles, I've known that quite a while," said the Angel stoutly.

"Mr. McLean told my father and he told me. That only makes me love you more, to pay for all you've missed."

"Then I'm wondering at you," said Freckles in a voice of awe. "Can't you see that if you were willing and your father would come and offer you to me, I couldn't be touching the soles of your feet, in love—me, whose people brawled over me, cut off me hand, and throwed me away to freeze and to die!

"I used to pray every night and morning and many times in the day to see me mother. Now I only pray to die quickly and never risk the sight of her."

His voice was raw as he cried:

"Oh, do, for mercy's sake, kiss me once more, and then be letting me go!"

"Not for a minute!" cried the Angel. "It's you that has the wilderness in your head.

"You till torture yourself with the idea that your own mother might have cut off that hand. Shame on you, Freckles! Your mother would have done this. . . ."

The Angel deliberately turned back the cover, slipped up the sleeve, and laid her lips on the scars.

"Freckles! Wake up!" she cried, almost shaking him. "Come to your senses! Be a thinking, reasoning man! You must be some sort of a reproduction of your parents, and I am not afraid to vouch for them, not for a minute!

"Mr. McLean says that you are the most perfect gentleman he ever knew, and he has travelled the world over. How does it happen, Freckles? No one at that Home taught you.

"That means that it is born in you, and a direct inheritance from a race of men that have been gentlemen for ages, and couldn't be anything else.

"Freckles, are you listening to me? Oh! Won't you see it? Won't you believe it?"

"Oh, Angel!" chattered the bewildered Freckles. "Are you truly meaning it? Could it be?"

"Of course it could," flashed the Angel, "because it just is!"

"But you can't prove it!" wailed Freckles. "It ain't giving me a name or me honour!"

"Before night," said the Angel, "I'll prove one thing to you: I can show you easily enough how much your mother loved you. I'll hire the finest detective in Chicago, and we'll go to work together. This isn't anything compared with things people do find out."

Freckles caught her sleeve.

"Me mother, Angel! Me mother!" he marvelled hoarsely. "Did you say you could be finding out today if me mother loved me? How? Oh, Angel! All the rest don't matter, *if only me mother didn't do it!*"

"Then you rest easy," said the Angel, with large confidence. "Your mother didn't do it! Mothers of sons like you don't do such things as that. I'll go to work at once and prove it to you.

"The first thing to do is to go to that Home where you were and get the little clothes you wore the night you were left there. I know that they are required to save those things carefully. We can find out almost all there is to know about your mother from them.

"Did you ever see them Freckles?"

"Yes," said Freckles.

The Angel literally pounced on him.

"Freckles! Were they white?" she cried.

"Maybe they were, once. They're all yellow with laying and brown with blood-stains now,"

said Freckles, the old note of bitterness creeping
in. "You can't be telling anything at all by them,
Angel!"

"Well, but I just can!" the Angel said positively. "I can see from the quality what kind of
goods your mother could afford to buy. I can see
from the cut whether she had good taste, and I
can see from the care she took in making them
how much she loved and wanted you."

"But how? Angel, tell me how!" Freckles
implored with trembling eagerness.

"Why, easily enough," said the Angel. "I
thought you'd understand. People that can afford
anything at all always buy white for new little
babies—linen and lace, and the very finest
things to be had.

"There's a young woman living near us who
cut up her wedding-clothes to have fine things
for her baby. Mothers that love and want their
babies don't buy rough, ready-made little things,
and they don't run up what they make on an old
sewing-machine.

"They make fine seams, and tucks, and put
on lace and trimming by hand. They sit and
stitch, and stitch—little, even stitches, every one
just as careful.

"Freckles, I'll wager you a dollar that those
little clothes of yours are just alive with the dearest, tiny hand-made stitches."

A new light dawned in Freckles' eyes. A
tinge of warm colour swept into his face, and renewed strength was noticeable in his grip of her
hands.

"Oh, Angel! Will you go now? Will you be
hurrying?" he cried.

"Right away," said the Angel. "I won't stay for a thing, and I'll hurry with all my might."

She smoothed his pillow, straightened the cover, gave him one steady look in the eyes, and went quietly from the room.

Outside the door, McLean and the Surgeon anxiously awaited her. McLean caught her shoulders.

"Angel, what have you done?" he demanded desperately.

The Angel smiled defiance into his eyes.

"What have I done?" she retorted. "I've tried to save Freckles."

McLean groaned.

"What will your father say?" he cried.

"It strikes me," said the Angel, "that what Freckles said would be more to the point."

"Freckles!" exclaimed McLean. "What could he say?"

"He seemed to be able to say several things," said the Angel sweetly. "I fancy the one that concerns you most at present was that if my father would offer me to him, he would not have me."

"And no one knows why better than I do," thundered McLean. "Every day he must astonish me with some new fineness."

He gripped the Surgeon until he almost lifted him from the floor.

"Save him!" he commanded. "Save him!" he implored. "He is too fine to be sacrificed."

"His salvation lies here," said the Surgeon, stroking the Angel's sunshiny hair, "and I can read in the face of her that she knows how she is going to work it out. Don't trouble for the boy. She will save him!"

The Angel laughingly sped down the hall and into the street, just as she was.

*   *   *

"I have come," she said to the Matron of the Home, "to ask if you will allow me to examine, or, better yet, to take with me, the little clothes that a boy you called Freckles, who was discharged last fall, wore the night he was left here."

The woman eyed her in greater astonishment than the occasion demanded.

"Well, I'd be glad to let you see them," she said at last, "but the fact is we haven't them. We let his people take those things away yesterday. Who are you, and what do you want with them?"

The Angel stood dazed and speechless, staring at the Matron.

"There couldn't have been a mistake," continued the Matron, seeing the Angel's pitiful distress.

"Freckles was here when I took charge ten years ago. These people had it all proved that he belonged to them. They had him traced to where he ran away in Illinois last fall, and there they completely lost track of him.

"I'm sorry you seem so terribly disappointed, but it is all right. The man is his uncle, and as like the boy as he could possibly be. He is almost killed to go back without him. If you know where Freckles is, they'd give big money to find out."

The Angel laid a hand along each cheek to steady her chattering teeth.

"Who are they?" she stammered. "Where are they going?"

"They are Irish folks, Miss," said the Matron. "They have been in Chicago and over the country for the last three months, hunting him everywhere. They have given up and are starting home today. They—"

"Did they leave an address? Where could I find them?" interrupted the Angel.

"They left a card, and I notice the morning paper has the man's picture and is full of them. They've advertised a great deal in the city papers. It's a wonder you haven't seen something."

"Please give me that card quickly. They may escape me. I simply must catch them!" snapped the Angel.

The Matron hurried to the secretary and came back with a card.

"Their addresses are there," she said. "Both in Chicago and at their home. You're sure to catch them before they sail—if you hurry."

The Matron caught up a paper and thrust it into the Angel's hand as she rushed for the street.

The Angel glanced at the card. The Chicago address was Suite Eleven, Auditorium. She laid her hand on the driver's sleeve and looked into his eyes.

"There is a fast-driving limit?" she asked.

"Yes, Miss."

"Will you crowd it all you can without danger of arrest? I will pay well. I must catch some people!"

The Hospital, an Orphans' Home, and the Auditorium seemed a queer combination to that driver, but the Angel was always and everywhere the Angel, and her methods were strictly her own.

"I will get you there just as quickly as any man could with a team," he said promptly.

Slamming the door, he sprang to the box and gave the horses a cut that rolled the Angel from her seat.

She clung to the card and paper, and, as best she could in the lurching, swaying cab, she read the addresses over.

"O'More, Suite Eleven, Auditorium.

"O'More," she repeated. "Seems to fit Freckles to a dot. Wonder if that could be his name. 'Suite Eleven' means that you are pretty well fixed. Suites in the Auditorium come high."

Then she turned the card and read on its reverse: Lord Maxwell O'More, M.P., Killvany Place, County Clare, Ireland.

The Angel sat on the edge of the seat, bracing her feet against the one opposite, as the cab pitched and swung round corners and passed vehicles.

Mechanically she fingered the paste-board and stared straight ahead. Then she drew a deep breath and read the card again.

"A Lord-man!" she said, and groaned despairingly. "A Lord-man! Bet my hoe-cake's scorched! Here I've gone and pledged my word to Freckles I'd find him some decent relatives that he could be proud of, and now there isn't a chance out of a dozen but he'll have to be ashamed of them after all. It's too mean!"

Tears of vexation rolled down the tired, nerve-racked Angel's cheeks.

"This isn't going to do," she said, resolutely wiping her eyes with the palm of her hand and gulping down the nervous spasm in her throat.

"I must read this paper before I meet Lord O'More."

She blinked back the tears and, spreading the paper on her knee, read:

After three months' fruitless search, Lord O'More gives up the quest of his lost nephew and leaves Chicago today for his home in Ireland.

She read on, and looked at the picture. The likeness settled it. It was Freckles over again, only older and elegantly dressed. There was not a chance to doubt.

"Well, I must catch you if I can," muttered the Angel. "But when I do, if you are a gentleman in name only, you shan't have Freckles; that's flat. You're not his father, and he is twenty. Anyway, if the law will give him to you for one year, you can't spoil him, because nobody could."

Then she said to her driver:

"Thank you; and wait, no matter how long."

Catching up the paper, she hurried to the hotel desk and laid down Lord O'More's card.

"Has my uncle started yet?" she asked sweetly.

"His Lordship is in his room," the clerk said, with a low bow.

"All right," said the Angel, picking up the card. "I thought he might have started. I'll see him."

"Show Her Ladyship to the elevator and Lord O'More's suite," he said, bowing double.

"Ah, thanks," said the Angel, with a slight nod, as she turned away.

"I'm not sure," she muttered to herself as the elevator sped upwards, "whether it's the Irish or the English who say 'Ah, thanks,' but it's probable he isn't either; and anyway, I just had to do something to counteract that 'All right.' How stupid of me!"

At the bell-boy's tap, the door swung open and the liveried servant thrust a card-tray before the Angel.

The opening of the door created a current and the curtain swayed aside. In an adjoining room, lounging in a big chair, with a paper in his hand, sat the man who was, beyond question, of Freckles' blood and race.

With perfect control the Angel dropped Lord O'More's card in the tray, stepped past his servant, and stood before His Lordship.

"Good-morning," she said with tense politeness.

Lord O'More said nothing. He carelessly glanced her over with amused curiosity, until her colour began to deepen and her blood began to run hotly.

"Well, my dear," he said at last, "what can I do for you?"

"I am not your 'dear,'" she said with slow distinctness. "And there isn't a thing in the world you can do for me. I came here to see if I could do something—a very great something—for you; but if I don't like you, I won't do it!"

Then Lord O'More did stare. Suddenly he broke into a ringing laugh. Without a change of attitude or expression, the Angel stood looking steadily at him.

There was a silken rustle, and then a beautiful woman, with cheeks of satiny pink, dark hair,

and eyes of pure Irish blue, moved to
Lord O'More's side, and catching his arm shook
him impatiently.

"Terence! Have you lost your senses?" she
cried. "Didn't you understand what the child
said? Look at her face!"

Lord O'More opened his eyes wide and sat
up. He did look at the Angel's face intently, and
suddenly found it so good that it was difficult to
follow the next injunction.

He rose instantly.

"I beg your pardon," he said. "The fact is, I
am leaving Chicago sorely disappointed. It makes
me bitter and reckless. I thought you were some
more of those queer, useless people who have
thrust themselves on me constantly, and I was
careless. Forgive me, and tell me why
you came."

"I will if I like you," said the Angel stoutly.
"and if I don't, I won't!"

"But I began all wrong, and now I don't
know how to make you like me," said His Lordship, with sincere penitence in his tone.

The Angel found herself yielding to his voice.
He spoke in a soft, mellow, smoothly flowing Irish
tone, and although his speech was perfectly cor-
rect, it was so rounded and accented, and the sen-
tences were so turned, that it was Freckles over
again.

Still, it was a matter of the very greatest importance, and she must be sure; so she looked into
the beautiful woman's face.

"Are you his wife?" she asked.

"Yes," said the woman, "I am his wife."

"Well," the Angel said judicially, "the Bird
Woman says no one in the whole world knows

all a man's bignesses and all his littlenesses as his wife does. Do you like him?"

The question was so earnestly asked that it met with equal earnestness. The dark head moved caressingly against Lord O'More's sleeve.

"Better than anyone in the whole world," said Lady O'More promptly.

The Angel mused a second, and then her legal tinge came to the fore again.

"Yes, but have you anyone you could like better, if he wasn't all right?" she persisted.

"I have three of his sons," came the quick reply, "two little daughters, a father, mother, and several brothers and sisters."

"And you like him best?" the Angel persisted with finality.

"I love him so much that I would give up every one of them with dry eyes, if by so doing I could save him," said Lord O'More's wife.

"Oh!" cried the Angel. "Oh, my!"

She lifted her clear eyes to Lord O'More's and shook her head.

"She never, never could do that!" she said. "But it's a mighty big thing to your credit that she thinks she could. I guess I'll tell you why I came."

She laid down the paper and touched the portrait.

"When you were only a boy, did people call you 'Freckles'?" she asked.

"Dozens of good fellows all over Ireland and the Continent are doing it today," answered Lord O'More.

The Angel's face lighted with her most beautiful smile.

"I was sure of it," she said winningly. "That's what we call him, and he is so like you; I doubt if any one of those three boys of yours are more so. But it's been twenty years. Seems to me you've been a long time coming!"

Lord O'More caught the Angel's wrists, and his wife slipped her arms round her.

"Steady, my girl!" the man said hoarsely. "Don't make me think you've brought word of the boy at this last hour, unless you know surely."

"It's all right," said the Angel. "We have him, and there's no chance of a mistake. If I hadn't gone to that Home for his little clothes, and heard of you, but had met you on the street, I would have stopped you and asked you who you were, just because you are so like him.

"It's all right. I can tell you where Freckles is; but whether you deserve to know—that's another matter!"

Lord O'More did not hear her. He dropped into his chair and covered his face so that she should not see his eyes.

Lady O'More hovered over him, tears running down her cheeks.

"Umph! Looks pretty fair for Freckles," muttered the Angel. "Lots of things can be explained; now, perhaps, they can explain this."

They did explain, so fully that in a few minutes the Angel was on her feet, hurrying Lord and Lady O'More to reach the Hospital.

"You said Freckles' old Nurse knew his mother's picture instantly," said the Angel. "I want that picture and the bundle of little clothes."

Lady O'More gave them into her hands.

The likeness was a large miniature, painted

on ivory, with a frame of beaten gold, and the
face that looked from it was of extreme beauty
and surpassing sweetness.

Surrounded by masses of dark hair was a
delicately cut face with big eyes. In the upper
part of it there was no trace of Freckles, but the
lips curving in a smile were his very own.

The Angel gazed at it steadfastly. Then with
a quivering breath she laid the portrait aside and
reached both arms for Lord O'More's neck.

"That will save Freckles' life and ensure his
happiness," she said positively. "Thank you, oh,
thank you for coming!"

She kissed and hugged him, and then the
wife who had come with him. She opened the
bundle of yellow and brown linen and gave only a
glance at the texture and work.

Then she gathered the little clothes and the
picture to her heart and led the way to the
cab.

Ushering Lord and Lady O'More into the re-
ception-room, she said to McLean:

"Please go call up my father and ask him to
come on the first train."

She closed the door after him.

"These are Freckles' people," she said to the
Bird Woman. "You can find out about each other;
I'm going to him."

And she was gone.

*   *   *

The Nurse left the room quietly as the Angel
entered.

When they were alone, the Angel turned to
Freckles and saw that the crisis was at hand.

His eyes flashed with excitement.

"Angel!" he said, panting. "Oh, Angel! Did you get them? Are they white? Are the little stitches there? *Oh, Angel! Did my mother love me?*"

"Yes, dear heart," she said, with fullest assurance. "No little clothes were ever whiter. I never in all my life saw such dainty, fine little stitches; and as for loving you, no boy's mother ever loved him more!"

A nervous trembling seized Freckles.

"Sure? Are you sure?" he urged, with clicking teeth.

"I know," said the Angel firmly. "And, Freckles, while you rest and be glad, I want to tell you a little story. When you feel stronger we will look at the clothes together. They are here. They are all right.

"But while I was at the Home getting them, I heard of some people that were hunting a lost boy. I went to see them, and what they told me was all so exactly like what might have happened to you that I must tell you.

"There was a sour, grumpy old man," she went on. "He always had been spoiled, because he had a title and a big estate. So when his elder son fell in love with a beautiful girl also with a title, that pleased him.

"Then he went and ordered his other son to marry a poky kind of a girl, that no one liked, to get another big estate on the other side of his.

"But that poor younger son had been in love with the village Vicar's daughter all his life. That's no wonder, for she could sing like the angels. She loved him to death too.

"The old man went to see the girl—and he hurt her feelings until she ran away. She went to London and began studying music.

"When the younger son found that she had left, he followed her and married her. But pretty soon things were going wrong.

"Winter came, it was very cold, and fuel for the fire was expensive. Rents went up, and they were expecting a baby—and they were almost distracted.

"So the man wrote and told his father all about it, and his father sent back his letter unopened and told him never to write again.

"When the baby came, there was mighty little left to pawn for food and a Doctor, and nothing at all for a Nurse; so an old neighbour woman went in and took care of the young mother and the little baby, just because she was so sorry for them.

"By that time they were way out in the suburbs on the top floor of a little wooden house, among a lot of big factories, and it kept growing colder, with less to eat.

"Then the man got desperate and he went just to find money somehow, and the woman was desperate too.

"She got up, left the old woman to take care of her baby, and went to the City to sing. The woman became so cold that she put the baby in bed and went home.

"Then a boiler blew up in a big factory beside the little house and set it on fire. A piece of iron was pitched across and broke through the roof.

"It came down, and smashed and cut just one little hand off the poor baby. It screamed and screamed, and the fire kept coming closer and closer.

"The old woman ran out with the other people and saw what had happened. She knew there wasn't going to be time to wait for the firemen, so she ran into the building.

"She could hear the poor little baby screaming, so she worked her way to him, and she found him hurt and bleeding.

"Then she was scared almost to death over thinking what its mother would do to her for going away and leaving him, so she ran to a Home for Friendless Babies that was nearby, and banged on the door.

"She hid across the street until the baby was taken in, and then she ran back to see if her own house was burning.

"The big factory and the little house and a lot of others were all gone. The people there told her that the beautiful lady had come back and run into the house to find her baby.

"She had just gone in when her husband came, and he went in after her, and the burning house collapsed on both of them."

Freckles lay rigidly, with his eyes on the Angel's face as she talked.

"Then the old woman was just sick about that poor little baby. She was afraid to tell them at the Home, because she knew she never should have left him alone.

"But she wrote a letter and sent it to where the beautiful woman, when she was ill, had said her husband's people lived.

"She told all that she could remember about the little baby: when he was born, how he was named for the man's elder brother, that his hand had been cut off in the fire, and where she had put him to be taken care of and doctored.

"She told them that his mother and father were both dead, and she begged and implored them to send someone to come and get him.

"You would think it would have melted a heart of ice, but that old man hadn't any heart to melt, for he got that letter, read it, and hid it away among his papers. He never mentioned it to a soul.

"A few months ago he died. When his elder son began to settle his business, almost the first thing he found was the letter.

"He dropped everything, and, with his wife, came to hunt for that baby. He always had loved his brother dearly, and when he had left he wanted him back.

"He had hunted for him all he dared all these years, but when he got here you were gone . . . I mean the baby was gone.

"I had to tell you, Freckles, for you see, it might have happened to you like that just as easily as to that other lost boy."

Freckles reached up and turned the Angel's face until he compelled her eyes to meet his.

"Angel," he said softly, "why don't you look at me when you are telling about that lost boy?"

"I . . . I didn't know I wasn't," the Angel said, faltering.

"It seems to me," said Freckles, his breath beginning to come in sharp wheezes, "that you got us pretty well mixed, and it ain't like you to be mixing things. If they were telling you so much, did they say which hand was off that lost boy?"

The Angel's eyes dropped again.

"It . . . it was the same as . . . yours," she ventured, barely breathing in her fear.

Still Freckles lay rigid and whiter than the coverlet.

"Would that boy be as old as me?" he asked.

"Yes," said the Angel faintly.

"Angel," said Freckles at last, catching her wrist, "are you trying to tell me that there is somebody hunting a boy that you're thinking might be me? Are you believing you've found my relations?"

Then the Angel's eyes came home. The time had come. She pinioned Freckles' arms to his sides and bent above him.

"How strong are you, dear heart?" she asked softly. "How brave are you? Can you bear it? Dare I tell you that?"

"No!" Freckles gasped. "Not if you're sure! I can't bear it! I'll die if you do!"

The day had been one unremitting strain for the Angel. Nerve-tension was drawn to the finest thread. It snapped suddenly.

"Die!" she flamed. "Die, if I tell you that! You said this morning that you would die if you didn't know your name and your people were honourable. Now I've found you a name, a mother that loved you enough to go into the fire and die for you, and the nicest kind of relatives. *You just try dying and you'll get a good slap!*"

The Angel stood glaring at him. One second Freckles lay paralysed and dumb with astonishment. Then the Irish in his soul rose above everything.

A roar of laughter burst from him. The terrified Angel caught him in her arms and tried to stifle the sound.

She implored and commanded.

The tears rolled from Freckles' eyes and he wheezed on. When he was too worn to utter another sound, his eyes laughed silently.

After a long time, when he was quiet, and rested, the Angel started talking to him softly. Her big eyes were humid with tenderness and mellow with happiness.

"Dear Freckles," she said, "there is the face of the mother who went into the fire for you, and I know the name . . . old and full of honour . . . to which you were born. Dear heart, which will you have first?"

Freckles was very tired, and big drops of perspiration ran together on his temples, but the watching Angel caught the words his lips formed:

"My—mother!"

She lifted the lovely pictured face and set it in the nook of his arm. Freckles caught her hand and drew her beside him, and together they gazed at the picture while the tears slid over their cheeks.

"My mother! Oh, my mother! Can you ever be forgiving me? Oh, my beautiful mother!" chanted Freckles over and over in exalted wonder.

He was so completely exhausted that his lips refused to form the question in his weary eyes.

"Wait!" cried the Angel, for she could no more answer that question than he could ask it. "Wait, I will write it!"

She hurried to the table, caught up the

Nurse's pencil, and on the pack of a prescription-tablet scrawled:

"Terence Maxwell O'More, Dunderry House, County Clare, Ireland."

"Angel, are you hurrying?"

"Yes," said the Angel, "I am. But there is a good deal of it. I have to put in your house and country, so that you will feel located."

"My house?" marvelled Freckles.

"Your uncle says your grandmother left your father her Dower house and estate, because she knew his father would cut him off.

"You get that, and all your share of your grandfather's property besides. It is all set aside for you and waiting. Lord O'More told me so. I suspect, Freckles, you are richer than McLean."

She closed his fingers over the slip and straightened his hair.

"Now you are all right, dear Limberlost Guard," she said. "You go to sleep and don't think of a thing but just pure joy, joy, joy! I'll keep your people until you wake up. You are too tired to see anyone else just now."

Freckles caught her skirt as she turned from him.

"I'll go to sleep in five minutes," he said, "if you will be doing just one thing more for me. Send for your father! Oh, Angel, send for him quick! How will I ever be waiting until he gets here?"

One instant the Angel stood looking at him. The next, a crimson wave rose up her lovely face. Her chin began a spasmodic quivering and tears sprang into her eyes.

Her hands caught at her chest as if she were stifling. Freckles' grasp on her tightened until he drew her beside him, then he slipped his arm round her and drew her face to his pillow.

"Don't, Angel; for the love of mercy don't be doing that," he implored. "I can't be bearing it. Tell me. You must tell me."

The Angel shook her head.

"That ain't fair, Angel," said Freckles. "You made me tell you when it was like tearing the heart raw from my breast. And you were for making everything Heaven—just Heaven and nothing else for me.

"If I'm so much more now than I was an hour ago, maybe I can be thinking of some way to fix things. You will tell me?"

He moved his cheek against her hair.

The Angel's head moved in negation. Freckles did a moment of intense thinking.

"Maybe I can be guessing," he whispered. "Will you be giving me three guesses?"

There was just the faintest possible assent.

"You didn't want me to be knowing my name?"

The Angel's head sprang from the pillow and her tear-stained face flamed with outraged indignation.

"Why, I did too!" she cried angrily.

"One gone," said Freckles calmly. "You didn't want me to have relatives, a home, and money?"

"I did!" exclaimed the Angel. "Didn't I go myself, all alone into the City, and find them, when I was afraid as death? I did too!"

"Two gone," said Freckles. "You didn't want the beautifulest girl in the world to be telling me—"

Beating in his brain past any attempted expression was the fact that, while nameless and possibly born in shame, the Angel had told him that she loved him.

"Angel," whispered Freckles, with his lips against her hair. "Angel, my darling little Swamp Angel, listen to me. If you don't want it that way, why, am I remembering anything?—not in my whole life!"

The Angel lifted her head and looked into the depths of Freckles' honest grey eyes, and they met her unwaveringly; but the pain in them was pitiful.

"Do you mean," she demanded, "that you don't remember that a brazen, forward girl told you, when you hadn't asked her, that she"—the Angel choked on it a second, but brought it out bravely—"that she . . . loved you?"

"No!" thundered Freckles. "No! I don't remember anything of the kind!"

But all the song-birds of his soul burst into melody over that one little clause: "When you hadn't asked her."

"But you will," said the Angel. "You may live to be an old, old man, and then you will."

"I will not!" cried Freckles. "How can you think it, Angel?"

"You won't even *look* as if you remember?"

"I will not!" persisted Freckles. "I'll swear to it if you want. I'd rather give it all up now and go into eternity alone, without ever seeing a soul of my same blood, or my home, nor hearing another man call me by the name I was born to, than to remember anything that would be hurting you, Angel."

The Angel's tear-stained face flashed into

dazzling beauty. A half-hysterical little laugh broke from her heart and bubbled over her lips.

"I'm so glad! Oh, I'm so happy! It's wonderful of you not to remember, Freckles, perfectly wonderful! It's not surprising that I love you so. The surprise would be if I did not. Oh, I so want to love you."

Pillow and all, she caught him to her breast for one long second, and then she was gone.

Freckles lay dazed with astonishment. At last his amazed eyes searched the room for something approaching the human to which he could appeal, and, falling on his mother's portrait, he set it before him.

"For the love of life! My little mother," he whispered, "did you hear that? Did you hear it! Tell me, am I living or am I dead and all Heaven come true this minute? Did you hear it?"

He shook the frame in his impatience at receiving no answer.

"You're only a pictured face," he said at last, "And of course you can't talk; but the soul of you must be somewhere, and surely in this hour you are close enough to be hearing.

"Tell me, did you hear that? I can't ever be telling a living soul; but, darling little mother, who gave your life for mine, I can always be talking of it to you!

"Every day we'll talk it over and try to understand the miracle of it!"

Then Freckles' voice ceased, his eyes closed, and his head rolled back from sheer exhaustion.

Later in the day he insisted on seeing Lord and Lady O'More, but he fainted before the resemblance of another man to him, and gave all his friends a terrible fright.

"Now, we are all going home," said the Angel to her father. "We have done all we can for Freckles. His people are here. He should get to know them. They are very anxious to become acquainted with him. We'll give him to them.

"When he is well, why, then he will be perfectly free to go to Ireland or come to the Limberlost, just as he chooses. Now, we will go at once."

McLean held out for a week, and then he could endure it no longer. He was heart-hungry for Freckles.

He started for Chicago, loaded with a big box of golden-rod, asters, fringed gentians, and crimson leaves, which the Angel had carefully gathered from Freckles' room, and a little, long, slender package.

He travelled with biting, stinging jealousy in his heart. He would not admit it even to himself, but he was unable to remain longer away from Freckles and leave him to Lord O'More.

As he entered Freckles' room he almost lost his breath. Everything was changed.

Freckles lay beside a window where he could follow Lake Michigan's blue until the horizon dipped into it. The room was filled with every luxury that taste and money could introduce.

All the tan and sunburn had been washed from Freckles' face in sweats of agony. It was a smooth white, its brown rift scarcely showing.

"Lord, Sir, but I'm glad to see you!" cried Freckles, almost rolling from the bed as he reached towards McLean.

"Tell me quick, is the Angel well and happy? Can Little Chicken spread six feet of wing and sail to his mother? How are all the gang? Have they found any more good trees?

"I've been thinking a lot, Sir. I believe I can find others near that last one. My Aunt Alice thinks maybe I can, and Uncle Terence says it's likely. Golly, but they're nice, elegant people. I'm proud to be the same blood with them!

"Come closer, quick! I was going to do this yesterday, and somehow I just felt that you'd surely be coming today, and I waited. I'm selecting the Angel's ring-stone.

"The ring she ordered for me is finished and they sent it to keep me company. See? It's an emerald—just my colour, Lord O'More says."

Freckles tilted a tray of unset stones that would have ransomed several valuable Kings. He held them towards McLean, stirring them with his right hand.

The diamonds joined the emeralds and pearls. There was left a little red heap, and Freckles' fingers touched it with a new tenderness. His eyes were flashing.

"I'm thinking this is my Angel's stone," he exulted. "The Limberlost, and me with it, grew in mine; but its going to bloom, and her with it, in this!

"There's the red of the wild poppies, the cardinal-flowers, and the little bunch of crushed fox-fire that we found where she put it to save me. There's the light of the campfire, and the sun setting over Sleepy Snake Creek. There's the red of the blood we were willing to give for each other.

"It's like her lips, and like the drops that dried on her beautiful arm that first day, and I'm thinking it must be like the brave, tender, clean red heart of her."

Freckles lifted the ruby to his lips and handed it to McLean.

"I'll be signing my cheque for you to have it set," he said. "I want you to draw out my money and pay for it with those very same dollars, Sir."

Again the heart of McLean took hope.

"Freckles, may I ask you something?" he said.

"Why, sure," said Freckles. "There's nothing you could ask that it wouldn't be giving me joy to be telling you."

McLean's eyes travelled to Freckles' right arm, with which he was moving the jewels.

"Oh, that!" cried Freckles with a merry laugh. "You're wanting to know where all the bitterness has gone? Well, Sir, 'twas carried from my soul, heart, and body on the lips of an Angel. It seems that hurt was necessary in the beginning to make today come true.

"The wound had always been raw, but the Angel was healing it. If she doesn't care, I don't. My dear future father-in-law doesn't, nor my aunt and uncle, and you never did.

"Why should I be fretting all my life about what can't be helped? The real truth is that since what happened to it last week, I'm so everlastingly proud of it that I catch myself sticking it out on display a bit."

Freckles looked the Boss in the eyes and began to laugh.

"You told me once on the trail, and again when we thought I was dying, that you loved me. Do these things that have come to me make any difference in any way with your feelings towards me?"

"None," said McLean. "How could they, Freckles? Nothing could make me love you more, and you never will do anything that will make me love you less."

"Glory be to God!" cried Freckles. "Glory to the Almighty! Hurry and be telling your mother I'm coming!

"Just as soon as I can get on my feet I'll be taking that ring to my Angel, and then I'll be making my start, just as you planned, only that I can be paying my own way.

"When I'm educated enough, we'll all—the Angel and her father, the Bird Woman, and you and me—all of us will be taking that trip together to see my house and my relations.

"When we get back, we'll add O'More to the name of the lumber-company, and golly, Sir, but we'll make things hum! Good land, Sir!

"Don't do that! Why, Mr. McLean, dear Boss, dear father, don't be doing that! What is it?"

"Nothing—nothing!"   McLean   choked. "Nothing—at all!"

He abruptly turned and hurried to the window.

"This is a mighty fine view," he said unsteadily. "The lake is beautiful this morning. But, Freckles, what is Lord O'More going to say to this?"

"I don't know," Freckles answered. "I am going to be cut deep if he cares, for he's been more than good to me, and Lady Alice is next to my Angel. She has made me feel that my blood and race are my own possession.

"She's talked to me by the hour of my father and mother and my grandmother. She's made them all so real I can lay claim to them and feel that they are mine.

"But nobody ever puts the width of the ocean between me and the Angel. From here to the Limberlost is all I can be bearing peaceably.

"I want the education, and then I want to work and live here in the country where I was born, and where the ashes of my father and mother rest.

"I'll be glad to see Ireland, and glad especial to see those little people who are my kin, but I'm not staying long.

"All my heart is the Angel's, and the Limberlost is calling every minute. You're thinking, Sir, that when I look from that window I see the beautiful water. No!

"I see mighty trees, swinging vines, bright flowers, and always masses of the wild roses, with the wild-rose face of my lady looking through.

"I see the swale rocking, smell the sweetness of the blooming things, and the damp, mucky odour of the swamp. I hear my birds sing, my squirrels bark, the rattlers hiss, and the step of Wessner or Black Jack coming.

"Whether it's the things that I loved or the things that I feared, it's all a part of the day.

"My heart's all my Swamp Angel's, and my love is all hers, and I have her and the swamp so confused in my mind I can never be separating them.

"When I look at her, I see blue sky, the sun rifting through the leaves, and pink and red flowers; and when I look at the Limberlost, I see a lovely face with blue eyes, gold hair, and red lips—and it's the truth, Sir, they're mixed till they're one to me!

"I'm afraid it will be hurting some, but I

have the feeling that I can be making my dear people understand, so that they will be willing to let me come back home.

"Send Lady O'More to put these flowers God made in the place of these glass-house ones, and please be cutting the string of this little package the Angel sent me."

As Freckles held up the package, the lights of the Limberlost flashed from the emerald on his finger. On the cover was printed:

"To the brave, wonderful, strong Limberlost Guard!"

Under it was a big, crisp, iridescent black feather.

"I love you!" Freckles whispered in his heart. "I worship you, my perfect Angel."

ABOUT THE EDITOR

BARBARA CARTLAND, the celebrated romantic author, historian, playwright, lecturer, political speaker and television personality has now written over 150 books. Miss Cartland has had a number of historical books published and several biographical ones, including that of her brother, Major Ronald Cartland, who was the first Member of Parliament to be killed in the War. This book had a Foreword by Sir Winston Churchill.

In private life, Barbara Cartland, who is a Dame of the Order of St. John of Jerusalem, has fought for better conditions and salaries for Midwives and nurses. As President of the Royal College of Midwives (Hertfordshire Branch), she has been invested with the first Badge of Office ever given in Great Britain, which was subscribed to by the Midwives themselves. She has also championed the cause for old people and founded the first Romany Gypsy Camp in the world.

Barbara Cartland is deeply interested in Vitamin Therapy and is President of the British National Association for Health.

BARBARA CARTLAND
PRESENTS
THE ANCIENT WISDOM SERIES

The world's all-time bestselling author of romantic fiction, Barbara Cartland, has established herself as High Priestess of Love in its purest and most traditionally romantic form.

"We have," she says, "in the last few years thrown out the spiritual aspect of love and concentrated only on the crudest and most debased sexual side.

"Love at its highest has inspired mankind since the beginning of time. Civilization's greatest pictures, music, prose and poetry have all been written under the influence of love. This love is what we all seek despite the temptations of the sensuous, the erotic, the violent and the perversions of pornography.

"I believe that for the young and the idealistic, my novels with their pure heroines and high ideals are a guide to happiness. Only by seeking the Divine Spark which exists in every human being, can we create a future built on the foundation of faith."

Barbara Cartland is also well known for her Library of Love, classic tales of romance, written by famous authors like Elinor Glyn and Ethel M. Dell, which have been personally selected and specially adapted for today's readers by Miss Cartland.

"These novels I have selected and edited for my 'Library of Love' are all stories with which the readers can identify themselves and also be assured that right will triumph in the end. These tales elevate and activate the mind rather than debase it as so many modern stories do."

Now, in August, Bantam presents the first four novels in a new Barbara Cartland Ancient Wisdom series. The books are THE FORBIDDEN CITY by Barbara Cartland, herself; THE ROMANCE OF TWO WORLDS by Marie Corelli; THE HOUSE OF FULFILLMENT by L. Adams Beck; and BLACK LIGHT by Talbot Mundy.

"Now I am introducing something which I think is of vital importance at this moment in history. Following my own autobiographical book I SEEK THE MIRACULOUS, which Dutton is publishing in hardcover this summer, I am offering those who seek 'the world behind the world' novels which contain, besides a fascinating story, the teaching of Ancient Wisdom.

"In the snow-covered vastnesses of the Himalayas, there are lamaseries filled with manuscripts which have been kept secret for century upon century. In the depths of the tropical jungles and the arid wastes of the deserts, there are also those who know the esoteric mysteries which few can understand.

"Yet some of their precious and sacred knowledge has been revealed to writers in the past. These books I have collected, edited and offer them to those who want to look beyond this greedy, grasping, materialistic world to find their own souls.

"I believe that Love, human and divine, is the jail-breaker of that prison of selfhood which confines and confuses us . . .

"I believe that for those who have attained enlightenment, super-normal (not super-human) powers are available to those who seek them."

All Barbara Cartland's own novels and her Library of Love are available in Bantam Books, wherever paperbacks are sold. Look for her Ancient Wisdom Series to be available in August.

Barbara Cartland

The world's bestselling author of romantic fiction. Her stories are always captivating tales of intrigue, adventure and love.